DEAD MAX COMIX

THE DEADENING

By Dana Sullivan

RED CHAIR
·PRESS·

Dead Max Comix is produced and published by:
Red Chair Press PO Box 333 South Egremont, MA 01258-0333
www.redchairpress.com

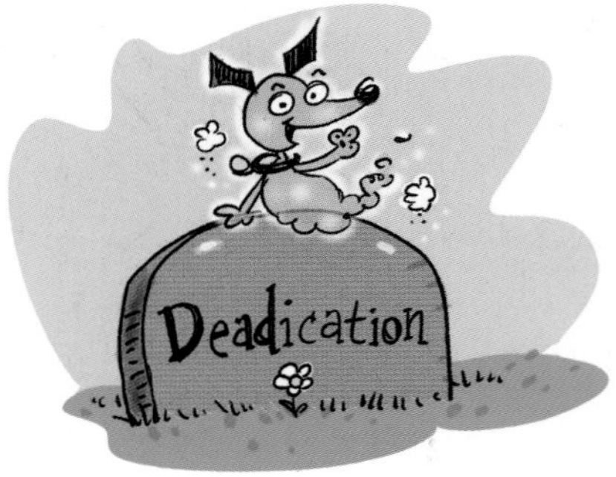
Deadication

To my three great dogs, past and present, Mike, Max and Bennie, and to all the dogs who bring unconditional love, joy, humor and clogged vacuums to their lucky humans around the world.

Publisher's Cataloging-In-Publication Data
Names: Sullivan, Dana, 1958- author, illustrator.
Title: The deadening / by Dana Sullivan.

Description: South Egremont, MA : Red Chair Press, [2020] | Series: Dead Max comix ; book 1 | Interest age level: 009-013. | Summary: "Derrick Hollis is a 7th grader at Zachary Taylor Middle School and an aspiring cartoonist too shy to show his work to anybody but his best friend Doug. Derrick is devastated when his dog Max dies. But after being cremated, Max returns from the other side and starts giving Derrick advice. Derrick could use it, especially when it comes to affairs of the heart and standing up to bullies."--Provided by publisher.

Identifiers: ISBN 9781634408523 (library hardcover) | ISBN 9781634408530 (paperback) | ISBN 9781634408547 (ebook PDF)

Subjects: LCSH: Middle school students--Comic books, strips, etc. | Dogs--Comic books, strips, etc. | Spirits--Comic books, strips, etc. | Bullying--Comic books, strips, etc. | CYAC: Middle school students--Cartoons and comics. | Dogs--Cartoons and comics. | Spirits--Cartoons and comics. | Bullying--Cartoons and comics. | LCGFT: Graphic novels.

Classification: LCC PZ7.7 .S85 2020 (print) | LCC PZ7.7 (ebook) | DDC 741.5973 [Fic]--dc23

LC record available at https://lccn.loc.gov/2019931706

Printed in the United States of America

09 1P CGBS20

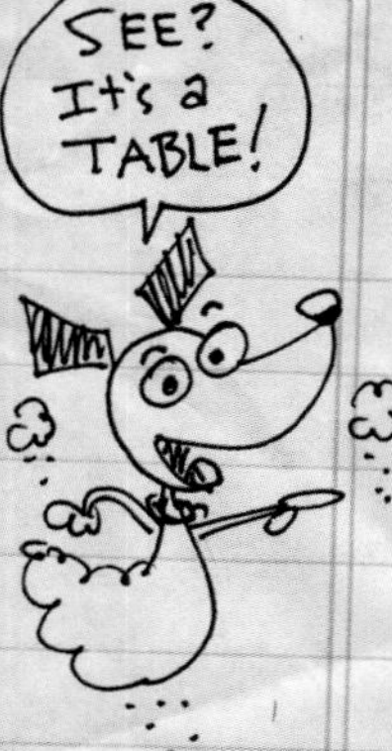
SEE? It's a TABLE!

Table of CONTENTS

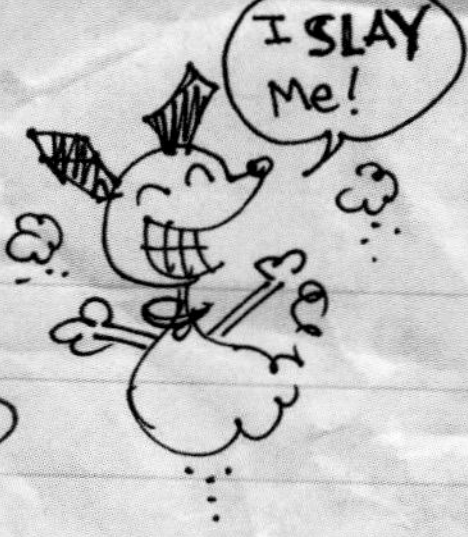
I SLAY Me!

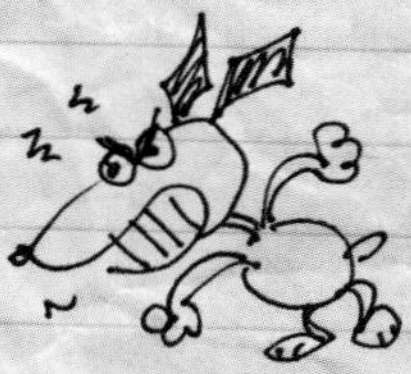

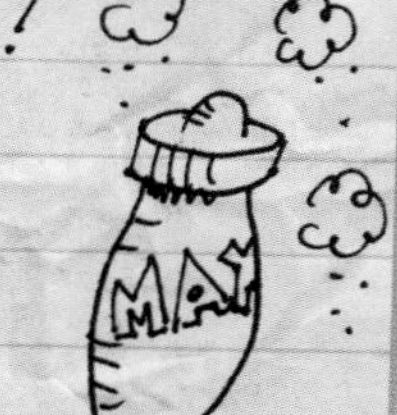
MAX

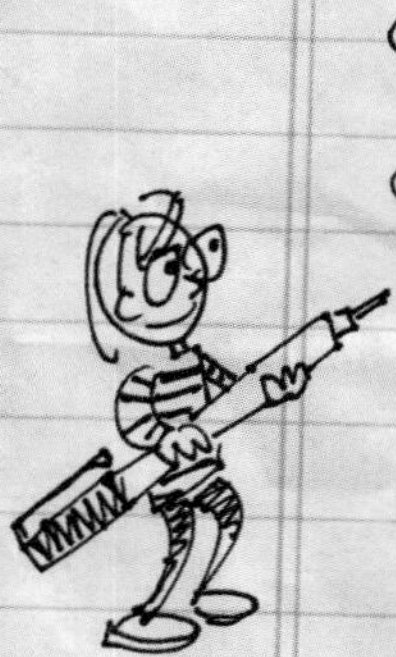

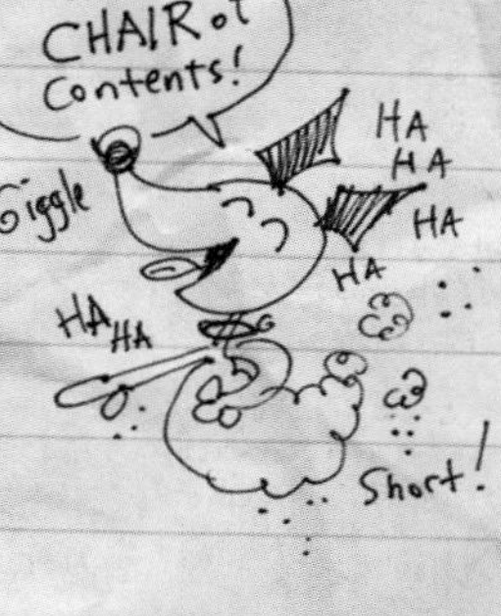
the CHAIR of Contents!
Giggle
HA HA HA
HA
HA HA
Short!

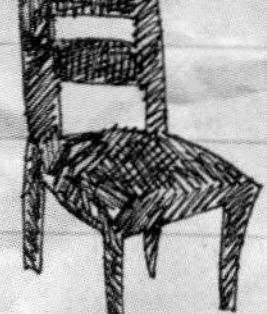

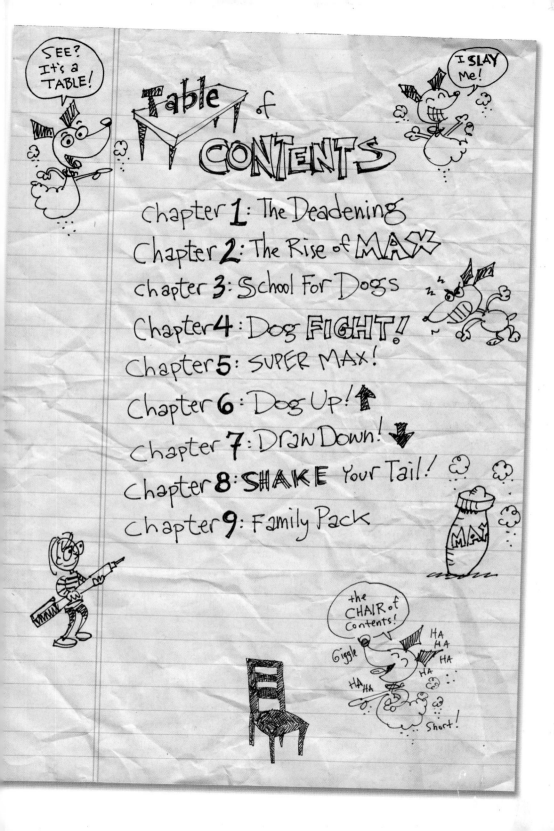

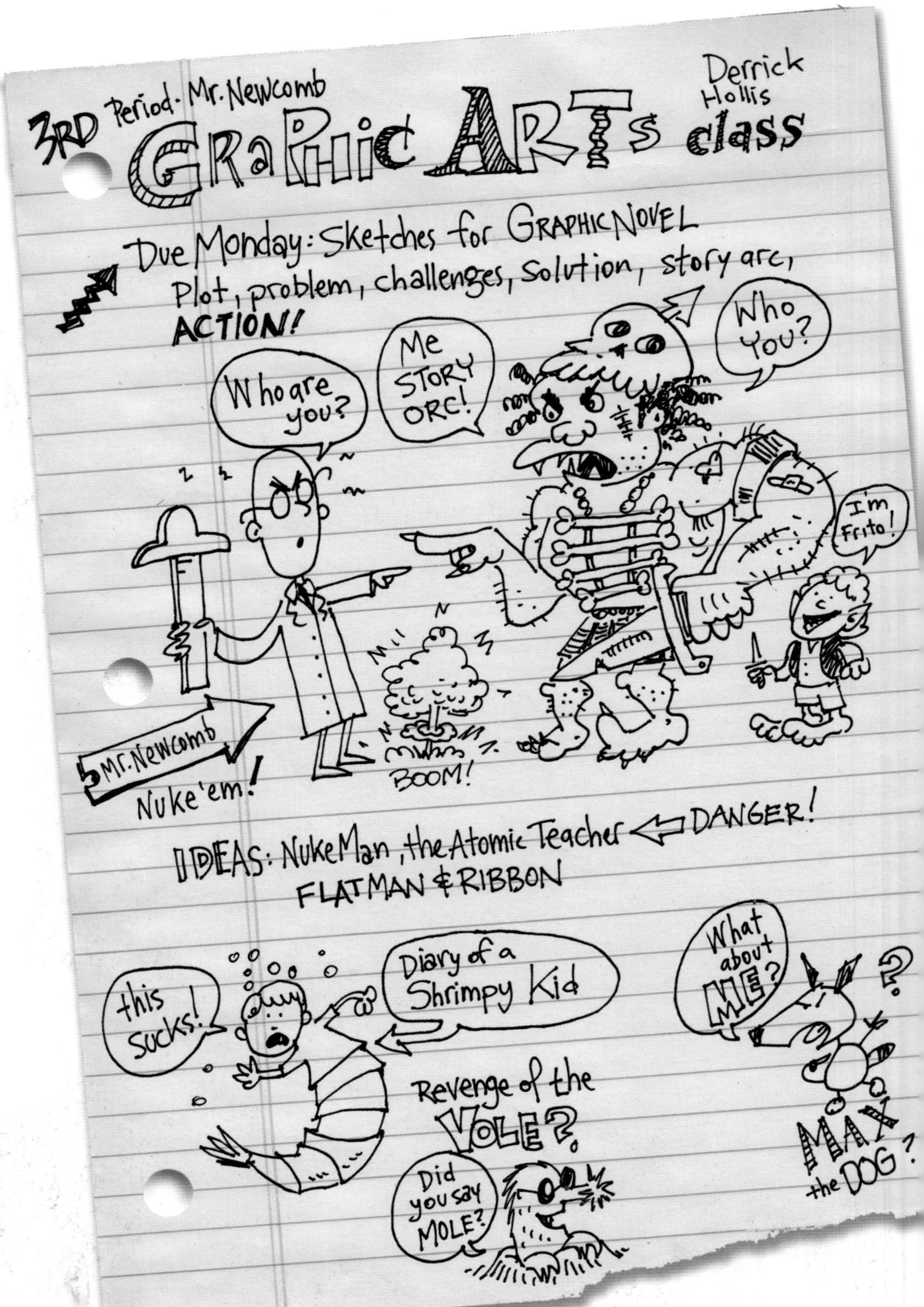

3RD Period · Mr. Newcomb
GRaPHIC ARTs class
Derrick Hollis
Due Monday: Sketches for GRAPHIC NOVEL
Plot, problem, challenges, solution, story arc,
ACTION!
Who are you?
Me STORY ORC!
Who YOU?
I'm Frito!
Mr. Newcomb
Nuke'em!
BOOM!
IDEAS: NukeMan, the Atomic Teacher ⇦ DANGER!
FLATMAN & RIBBON
this sucks!
Diary of a Shrimpy Kid
What about ME?
Revenge of the VOLE?
Did you say MOLE?
MAX the DOG?

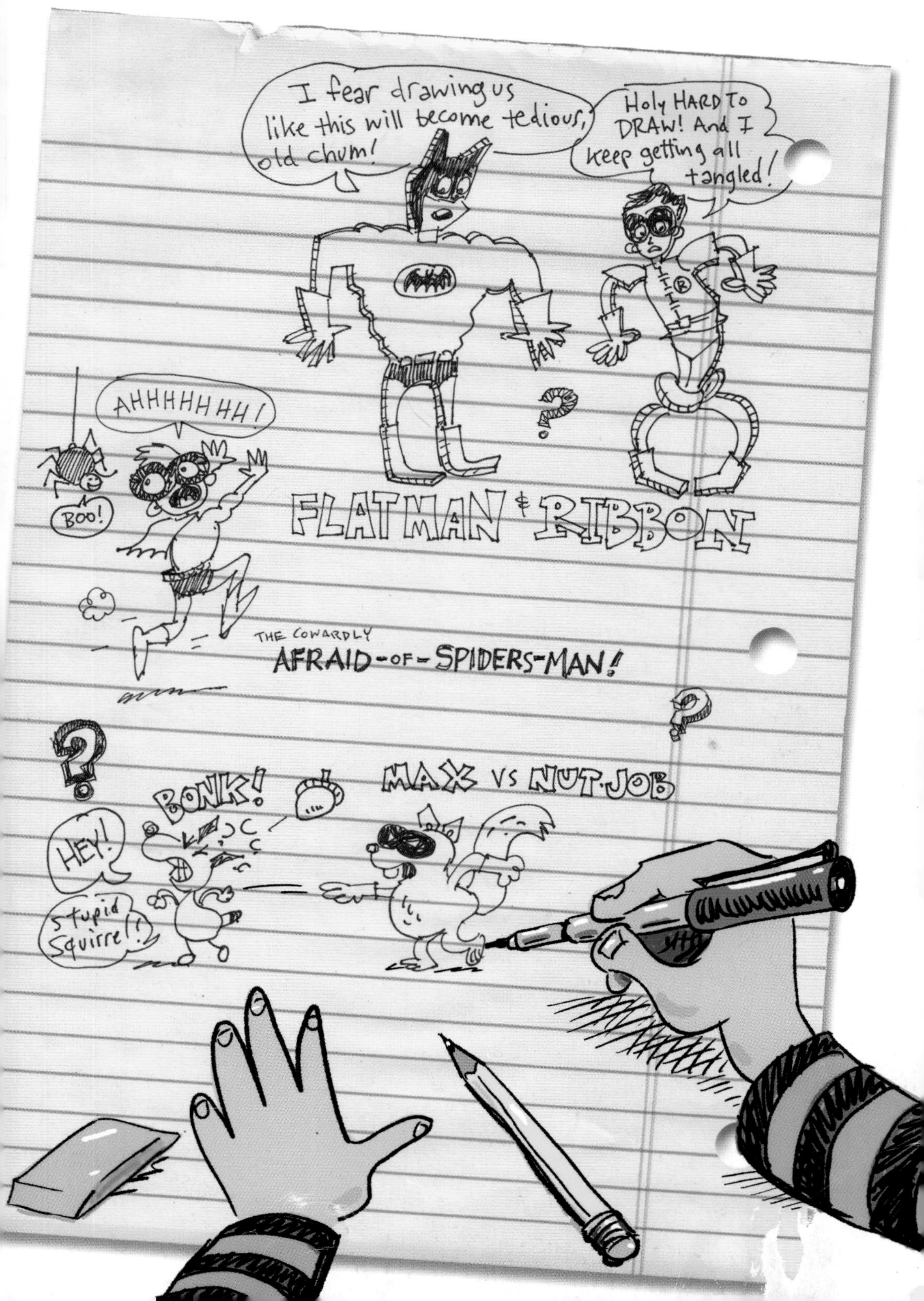

I fear drawing us like this will become tedious, old chum!
Holy HARD TO DRAW! And I keep getting all tangled!
FLATMAN & RIBBON
AHHHHHHH!
BOO!
THE COWARDLY
AFRAID-OF-SPIDERS-MAN!
MAX VS NUT-JOB
BONK!
HEY!
Stupid Squirrel!

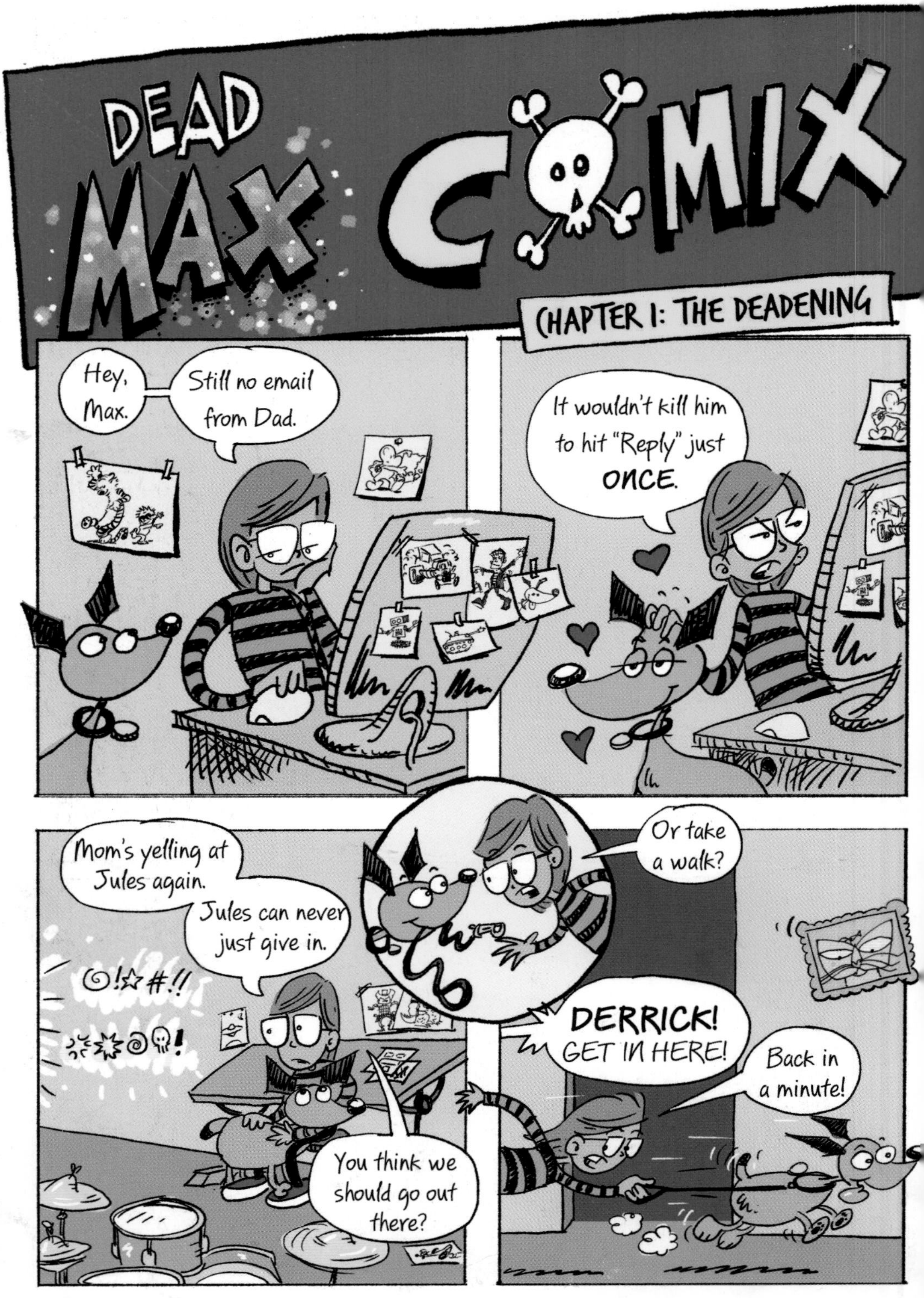

DEAD MAX COMIX
CHAPTER 1: THE DEADENING
Hey, Max.
Still no email from Dad.
It wouldn't kill him to hit "Reply" just ONCE.
Mom's yelling at Jules again.
Jules can never just give in.
You think we should go out there?
Or take a walk?
DERRICK! GET IN HERE!
Back in a minute!

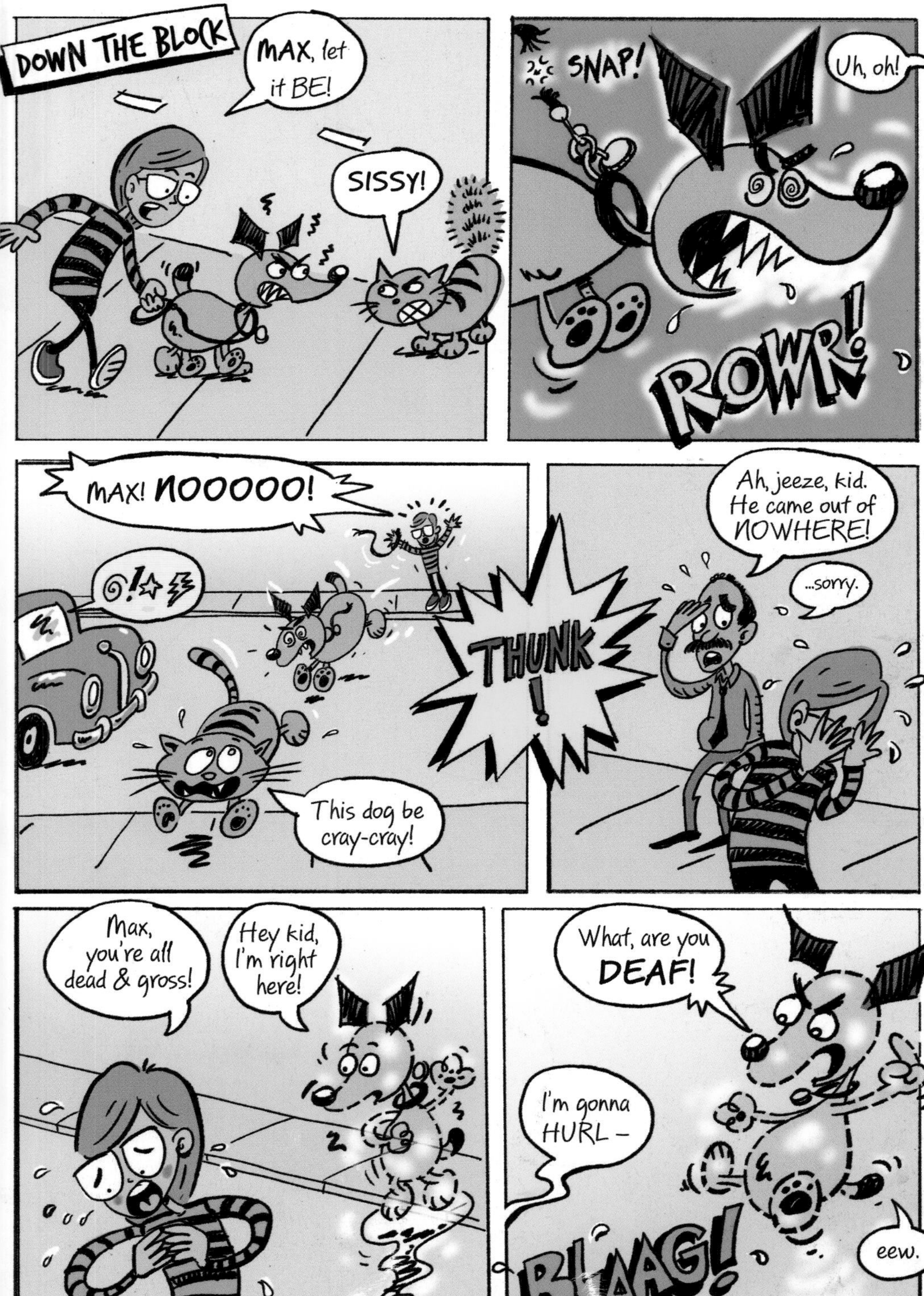
DOWN THE BLOCK
MAX, let it BE!
SISSY!
SNAP!
Uh, oh!
ROWR!
MAX! NOOOOO!
THUNK!
This dog be cray-cray!
Ah, jeeze, kid. He came out of NOWHERE!
...sorry.
Max, you're all dead & gross!
Hey kid, I'm right here!
What, are you DEAF!
I'm gonna HURL –
BLAAG!
eew.

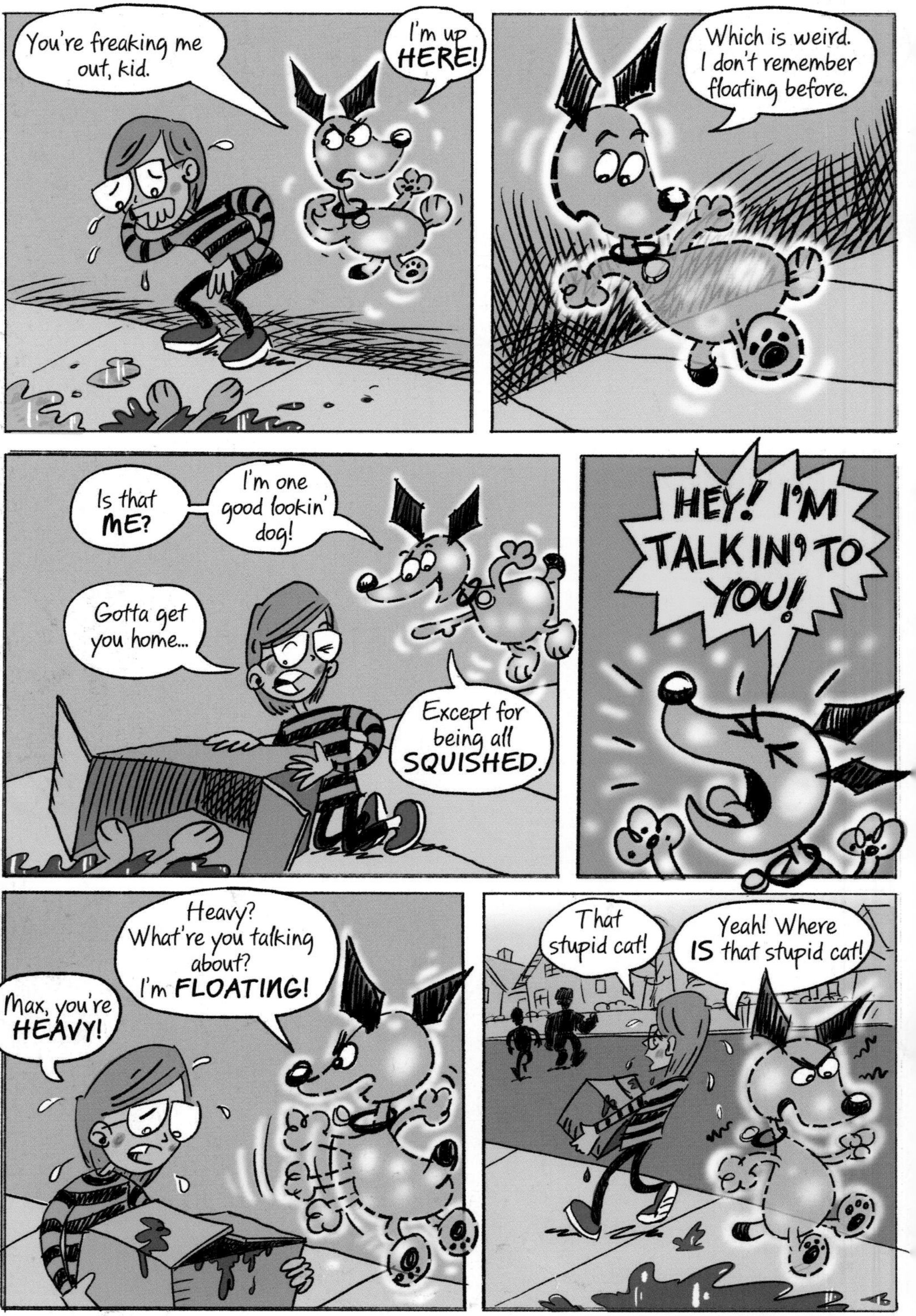
You're freaking me out, kid.
I'm up HERE!
Which is weird. I don't remember floating before.
Is that ME?
I'm one good lookin' dog!
Gotta get you home...
Except for being all SQUISHED.
HEY! I'M TALKIN' TO YOU!
Max, you're HEAVY!
Heavy? What're you talking about? I'm FLOATING!
That stupid cat!
Yeah! Where IS that stupid cat!

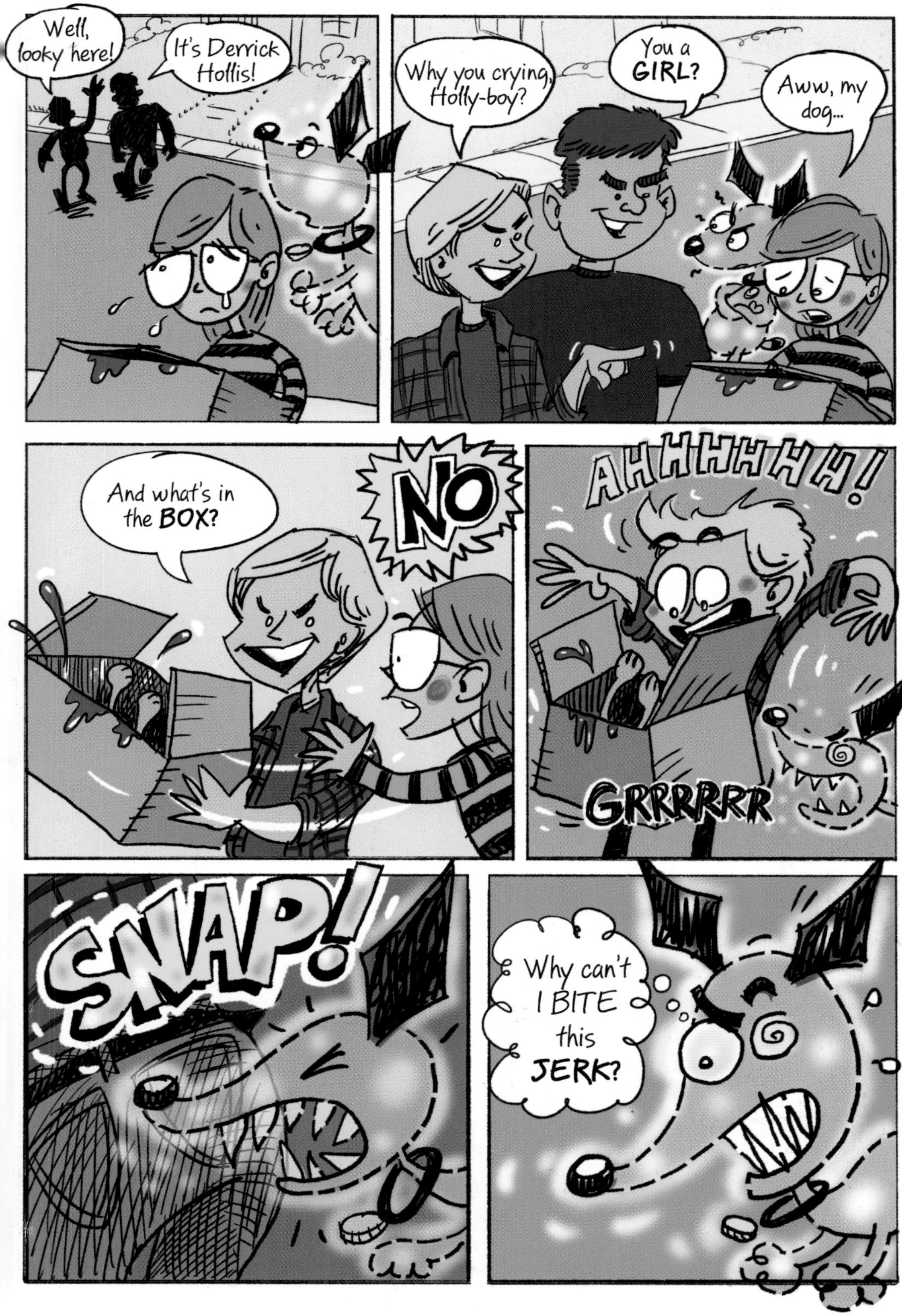

Well, looky here!
It's Derrick Hollis!
Why you crying, Holly-boy?
You a GIRL?
Aww, my dog...
And what's in the BOX?
NO
AHHHHHH!
GRRRRRR
SNAP!
Why can't I BITE this JERK?

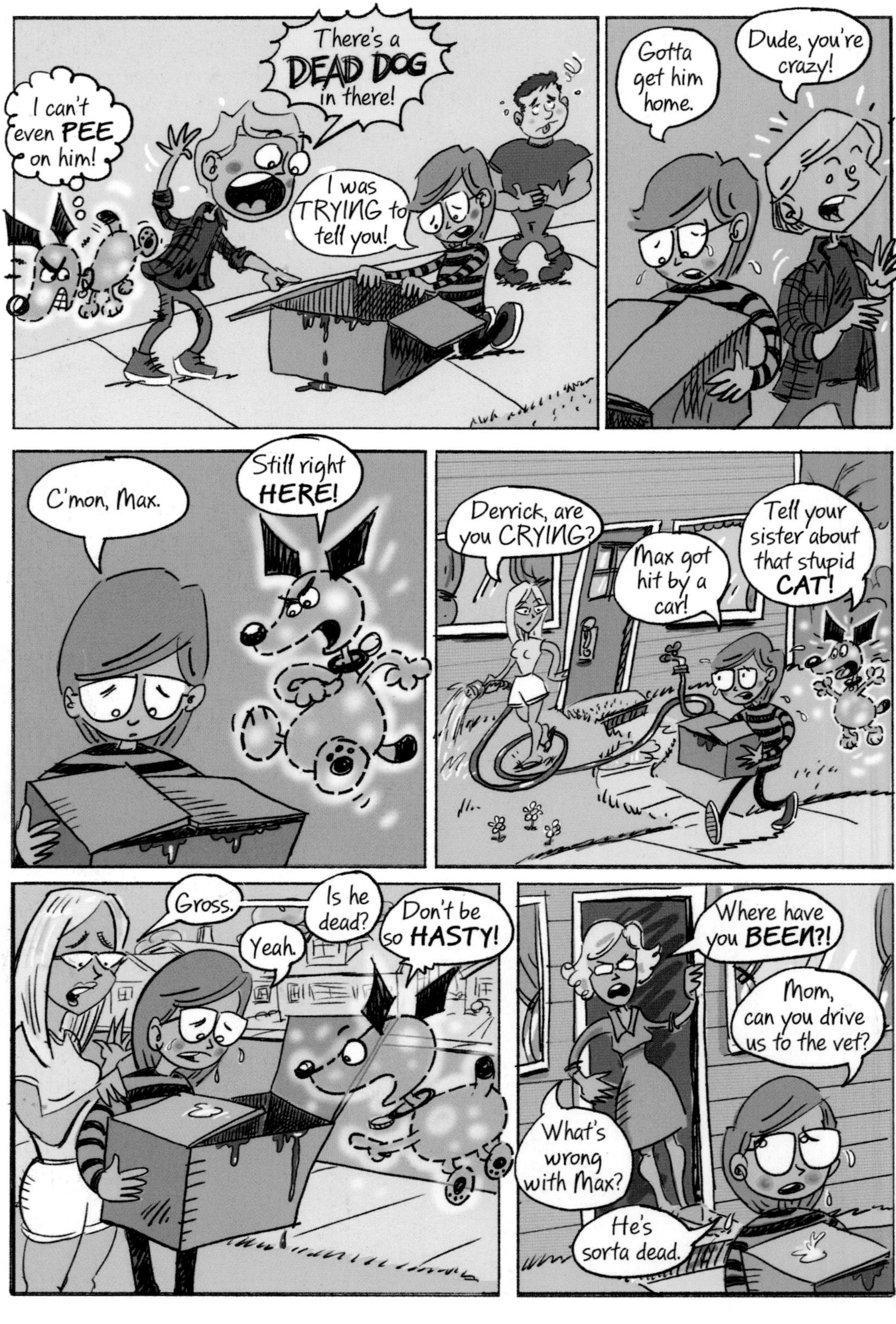

I can't even PEE on him!
There's a DEAD DOG in there!
I was TRYING to tell you!
Gotta get him home.
Dude, you're crazy!
C'mon, Max.
Still right HERE!
Derrick, are you CRYING?
Max got hit by a car!
Tell your sister about that stupid CAT!
Gross.
Is he dead?
Yeah.
Don't be so HASTY!
Where have you BEEN?!
Mom, can you drive us to the vet?
What's wrong with Max?
He's sorta dead.

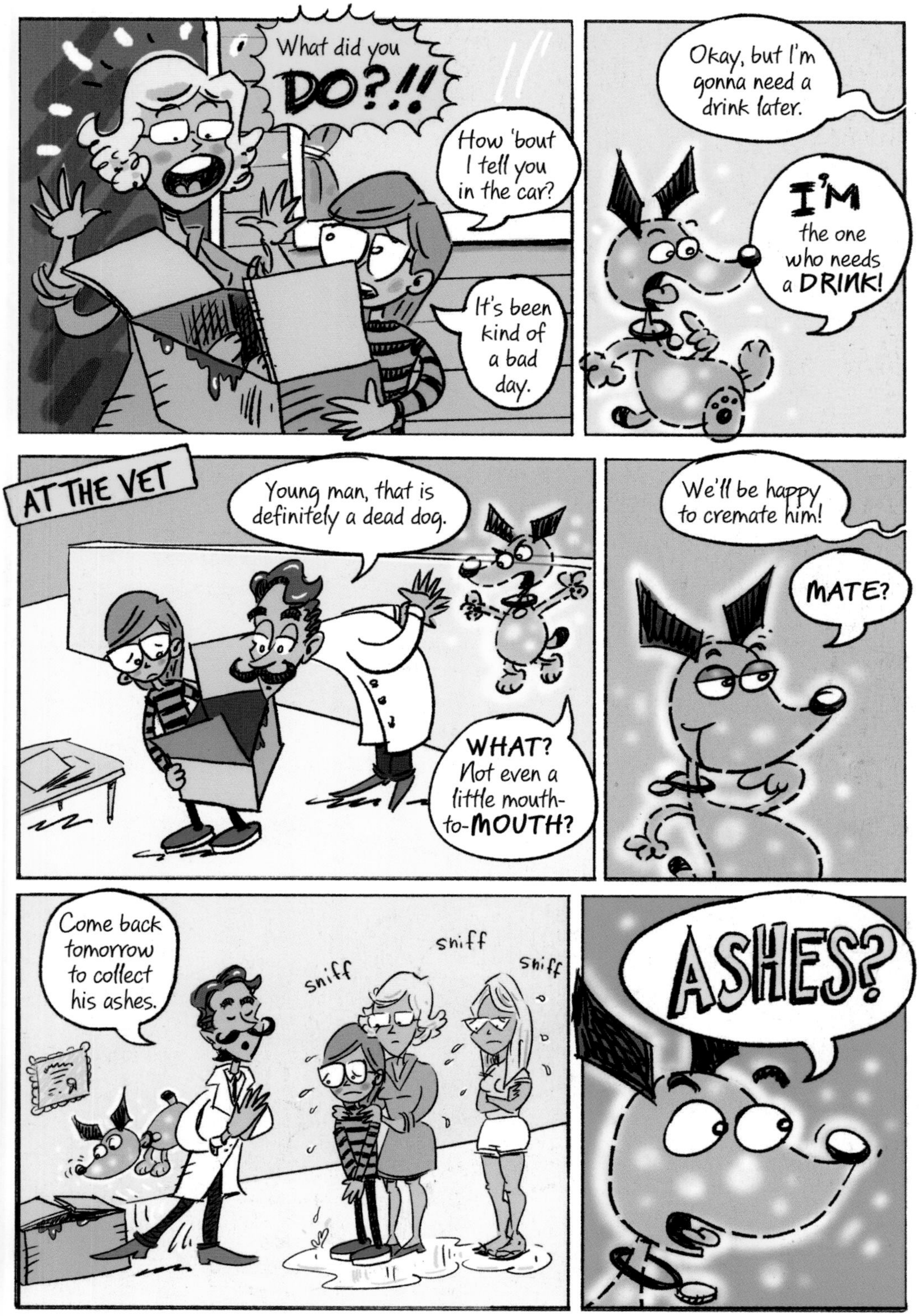
What did you DO?!!
How 'bout I tell you in the car?
It's been kind of a bad day.
Okay, but I'm gonna need a drink later.
I'M the one who needs a DRINK!
AT THE VET
Young man, that is definitely a dead dog.
WHAT? Not even a little mouth-to-MOUTH?
We'll be happy to cremate him!
MATE?
Come back tomorrow to collect his ashes.
sniff
sniff
sniff
ASHES?

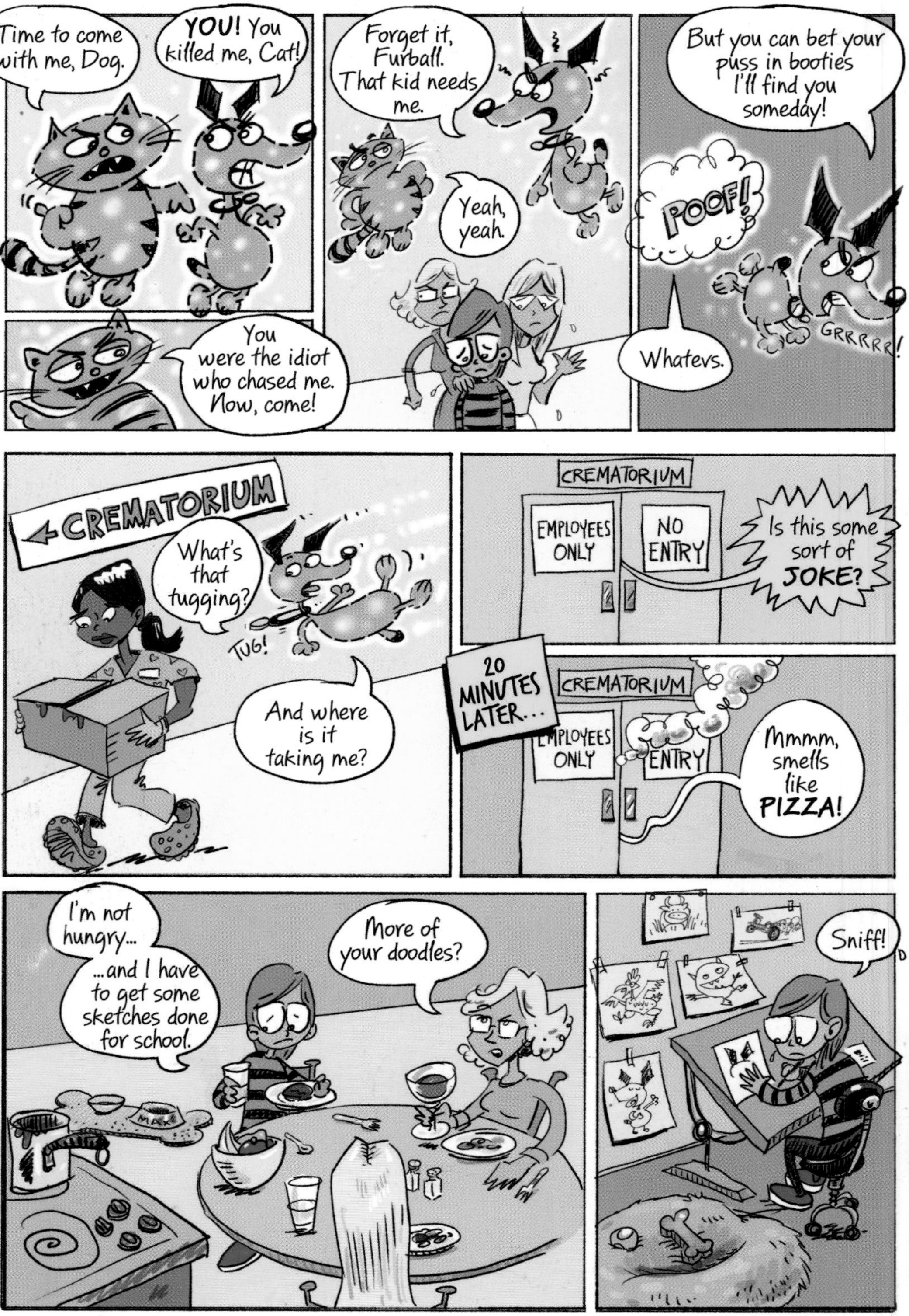

Time to come with me, Dog.
YOU! You killed me, Cat!
You were the idiot who chased me. Now, come!
Forget it, Furball. That kid needs me.
Yeah, yeah.
But you can bet your puss in booties I'll find you someday!
POOF!
Whatevs.
GRRRRRR!
CREMATORIUM
What's that tugging?
TUG!
And where is it taking me?
CREMATORIUM
EMPLOYEES ONLY
NO ENTRY
Is this some sort of JOKE?
20 MINUTES LATER...
CREMATORIUM
EMPLOYEES ONLY
ENTRY
Mmmm, smells like PIZZA!
I'm not hungry...
...and I have to get some sketches done for school.
More of your doodles?
MAX
Sniff!

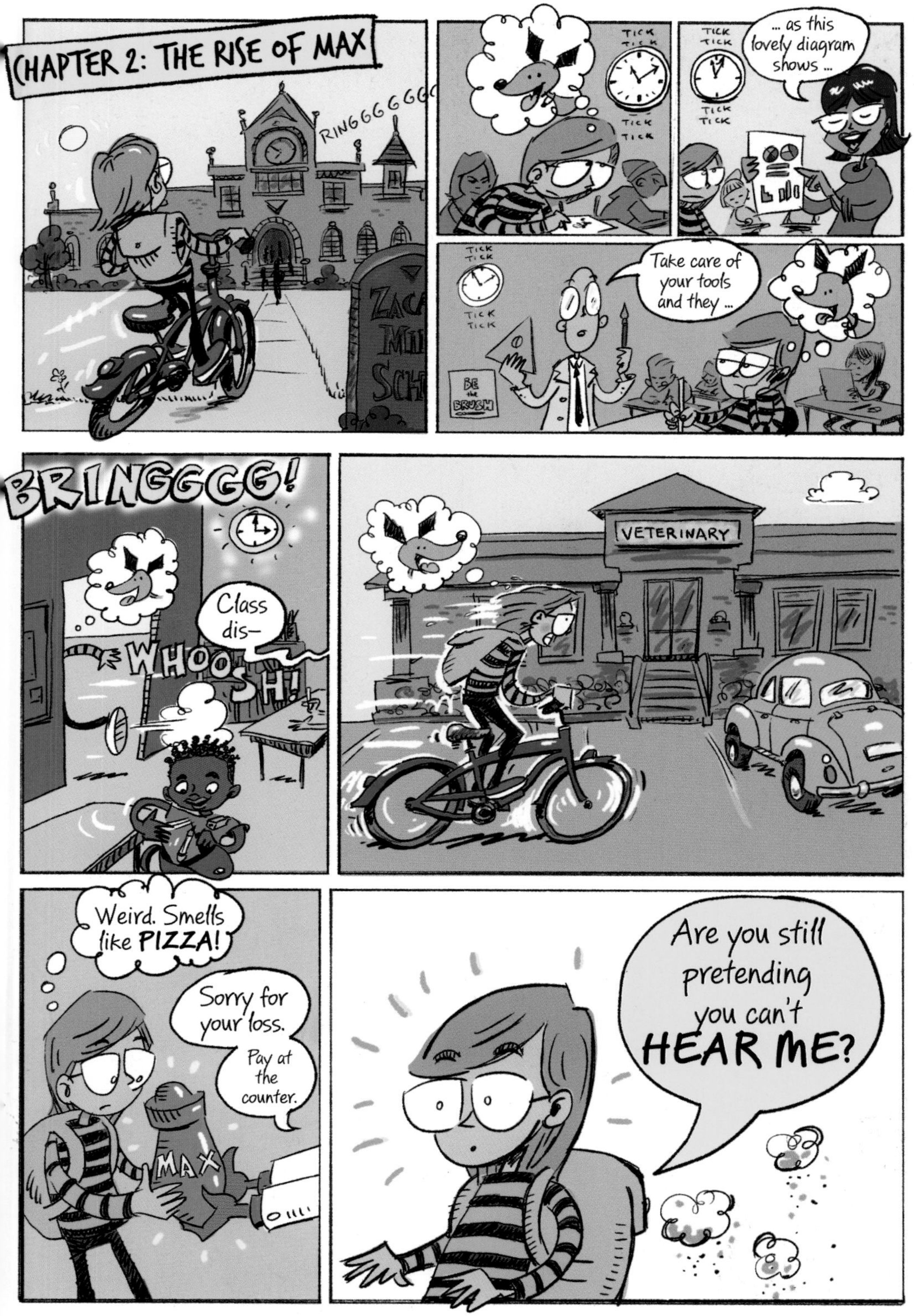
CHAPTER 2: THE RISE OF MAX
RINGGGGGGG
TICK TICK
TICK TICK
TICK TICK
TICK TICK
... as this lovely diagram shows ...
TICK TICK
TICK TICK
Take care of your tools and they ...
BE the BRUSH
BRINGGGG!
Class dis—
WHOOSH!
VETERINARY
Weird. Smells like PIZZA!
Sorry for your loss.
Pay at the counter.
MAX
Are you still pretending you can't HEAR ME?

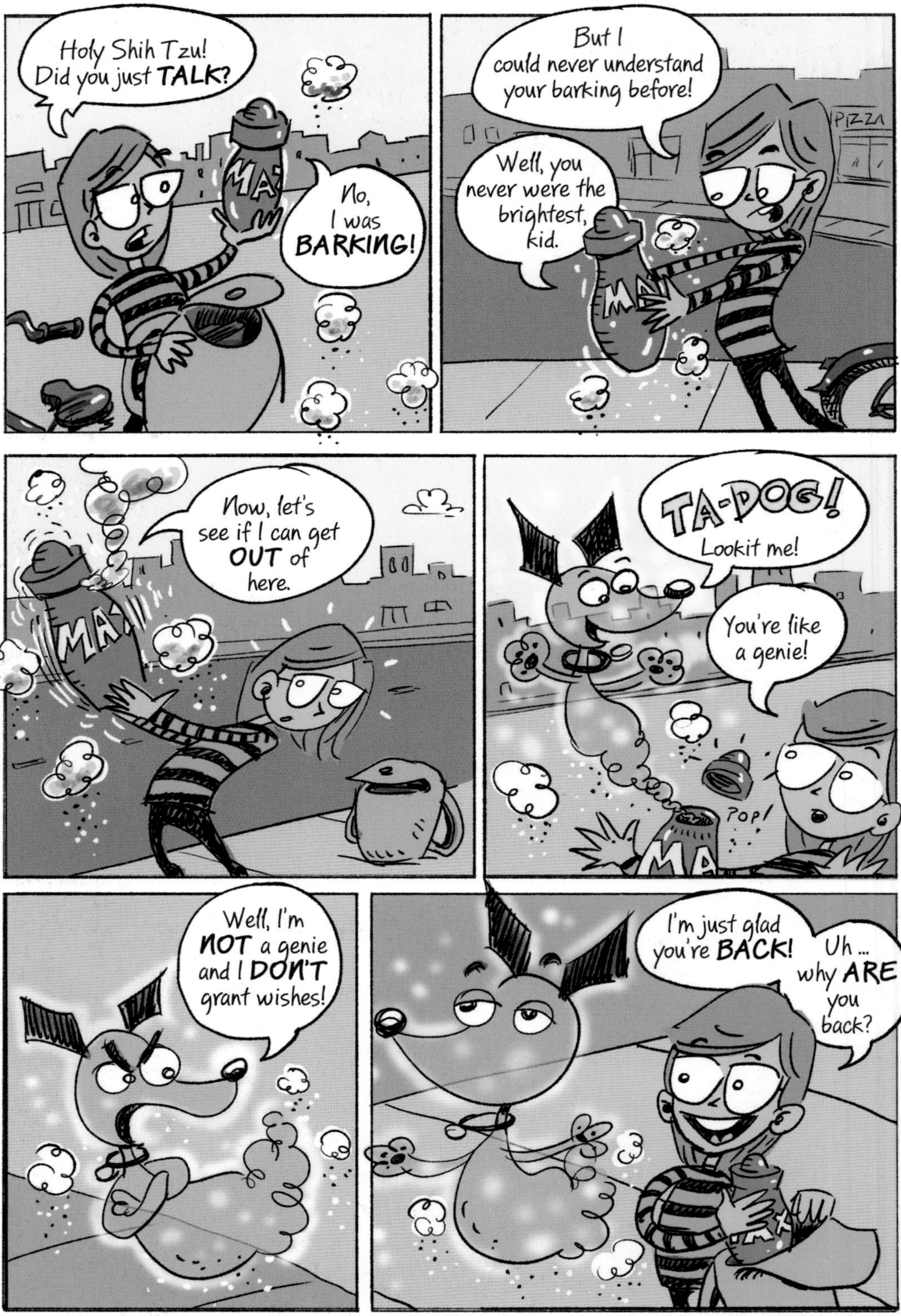
Holy Shih Tzu! Did you just TALK?
No, I was BARKING!
But I could never understand your barking before!
Well, you never were the brightest, kid.
PIZZA
Now, let's see if I can get OUT of here.
TA-DOG! Lookit me!
You're like a genie!
POP!
Well, I'm NOT a genie and I DON'T grant wishes!
I'm just glad you're BACK!
Uh ... why ARE you back?

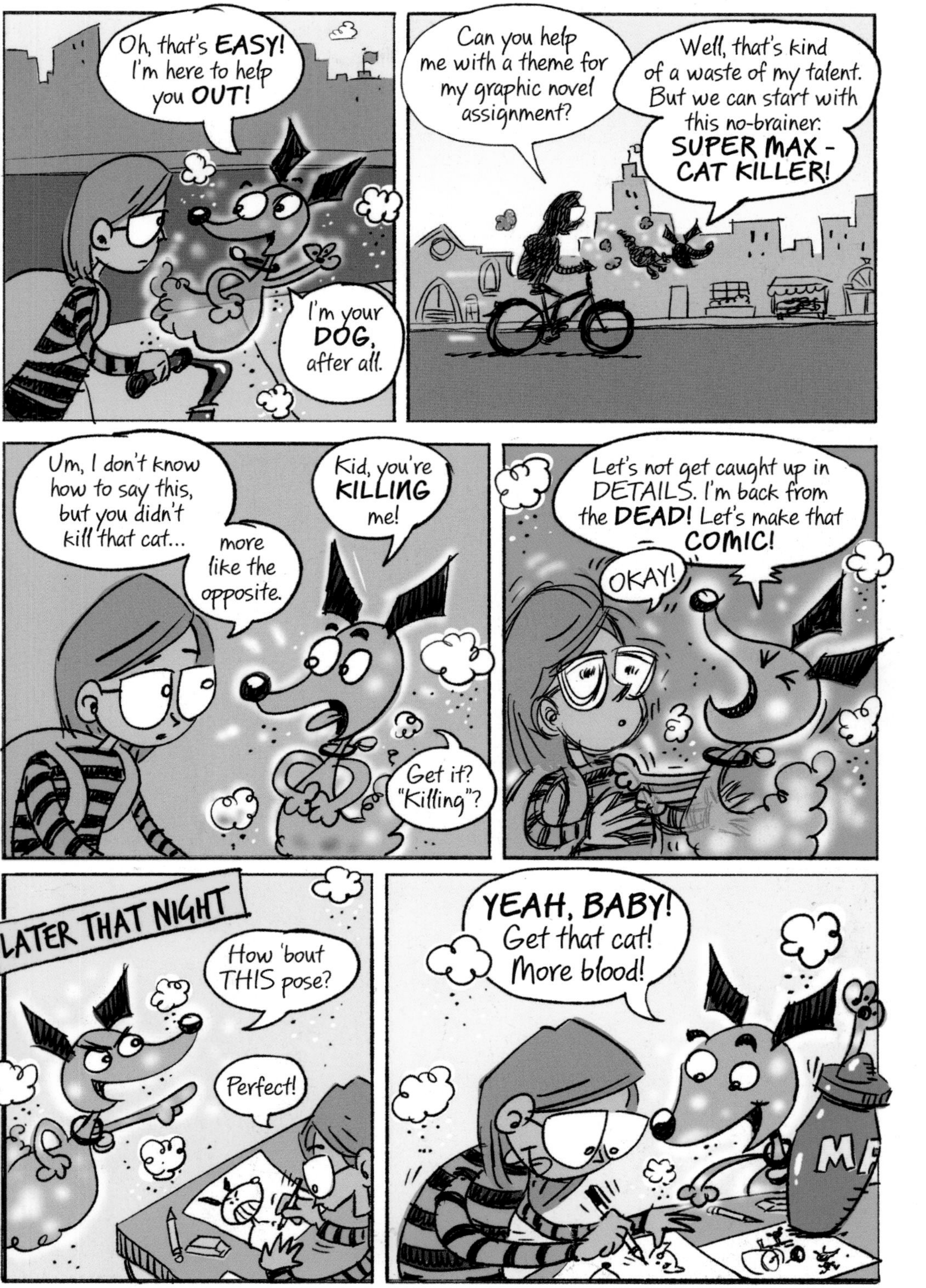
Oh, that's **EASY!** I'm here to help you **OUT!**
I'm your **DOG,** after all.
Can you help me with a theme for my graphic novel assignment?
Well, that's kind of a waste of my talent. But we can start with this no-brainer: **SUPER MAX - CAT KILLER!**
Um, I don't know how to say this, but you didn't kill that cat...
more like the opposite.
Kid, you're **KILLING** me!
Get it? "Killing"?
Let's not get caught up in DETAILS. I'm back from the **DEAD!** Let's make that **COMIC!**
OKAY!
LATER THAT NIGHT
How 'bout THIS pose?
Perfect!
YEAH, BABY! Get that cat! More blood!

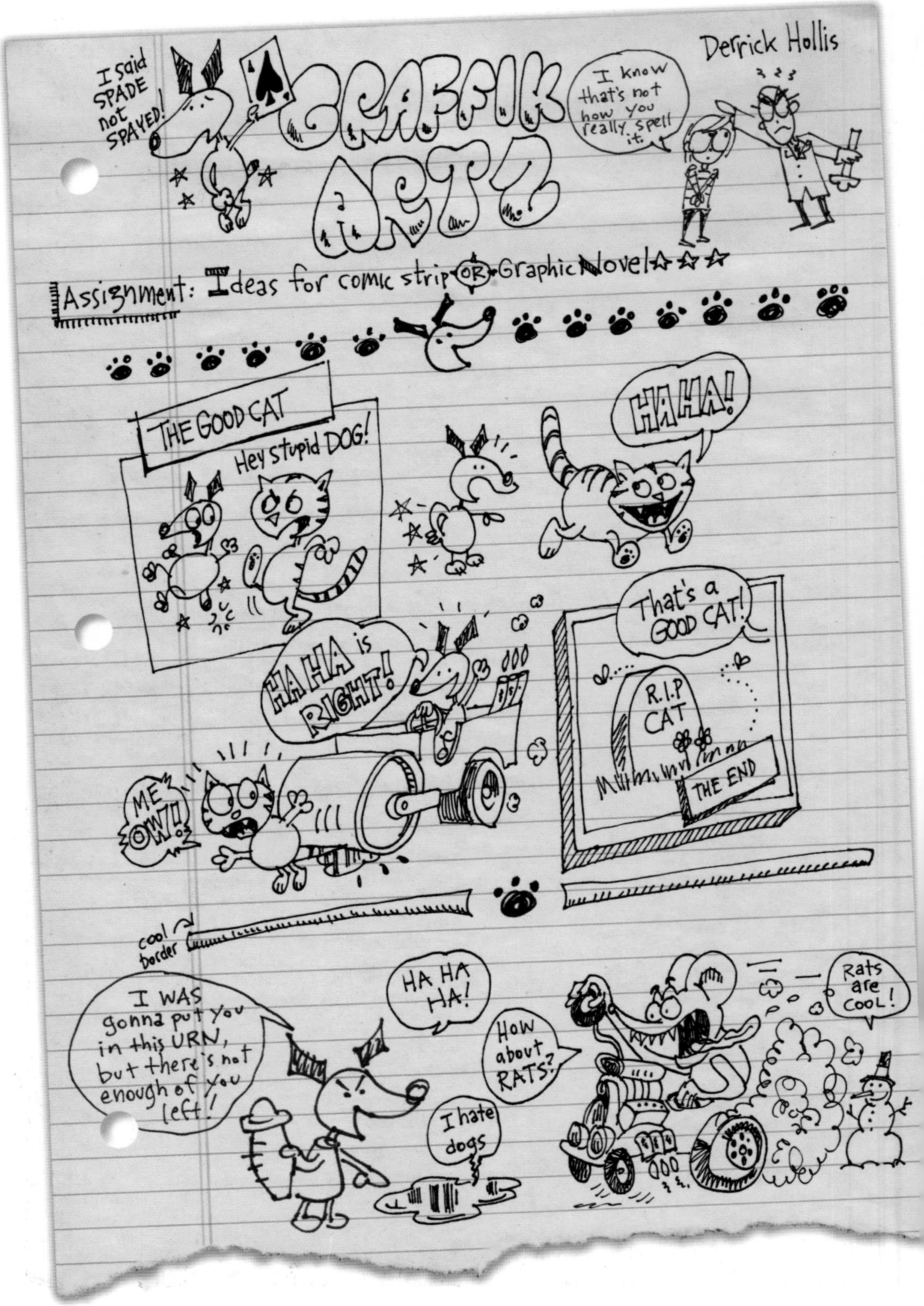

Derrick Hollis
I said SPADE not SPAYED!
GRAFFIK ARTZ
I know that's not how you really spell it.
Assignment: Ideas for comic strip OR Graphic Novel
THE GOOD CAT
Hey stupid DOG!
HAHA!
HA HA is RIGHT!
ME OW!!
That's a GOOD CAT!
R.I.P CAT
THE END
cool border
I WAS gonna put you in this URN, but there's not enough of you left!
HA HA HA!
How about RATS?
I hate dogs
Rats are COOL!

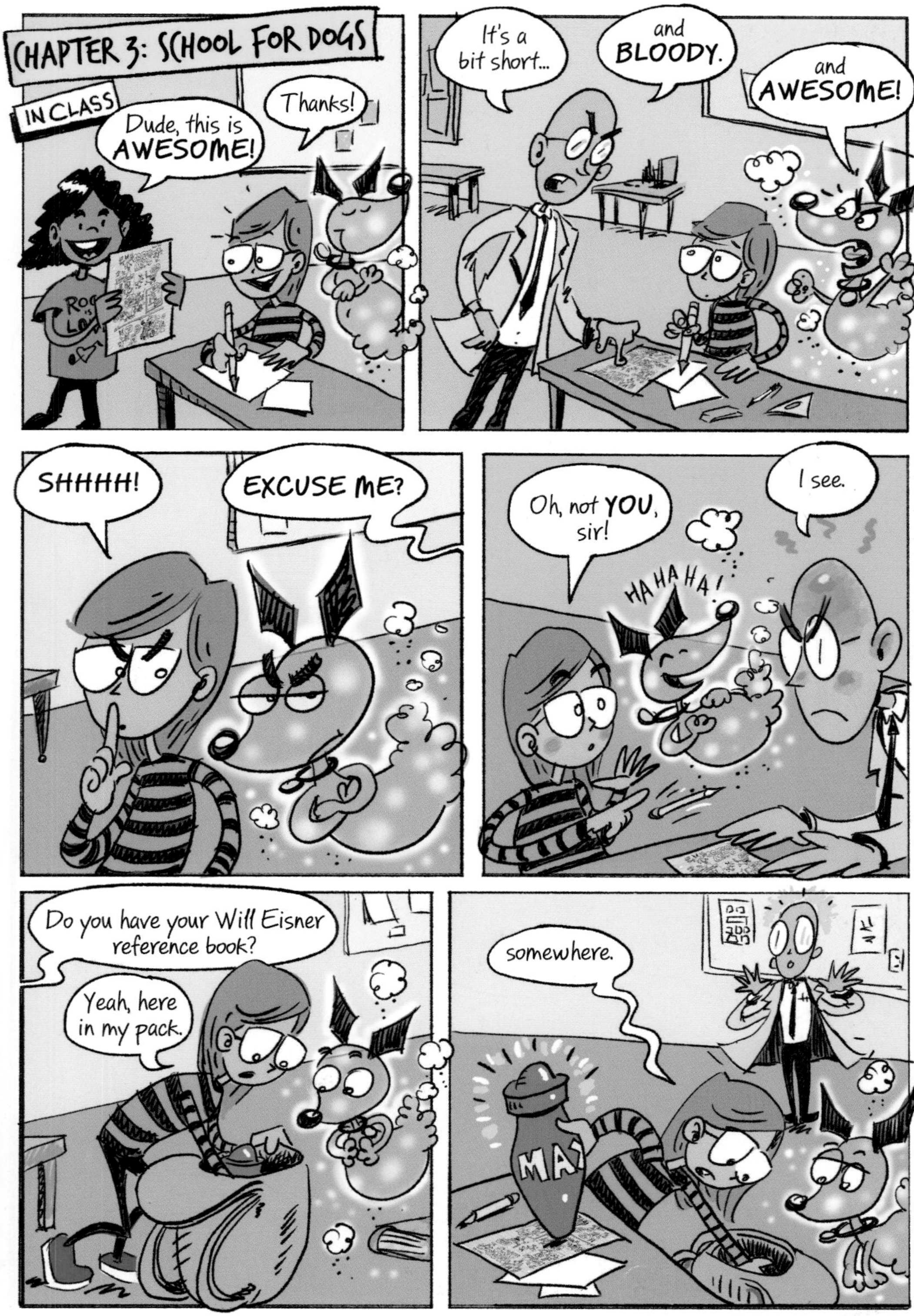

CHAPTER 3: SCHOOL FOR DOGS
IN CLASS
Dude, this is AWESOME!
Thanks!
It's a bit short...
and BLOODY.
and AWESOME!
SHHHH!
EXCUSE ME?
Oh, not YOU, sir!
I see.
HA HA HA!
Do you have your Will Eisner reference book?
Yeah, here in my pack.
somewhere.
MA

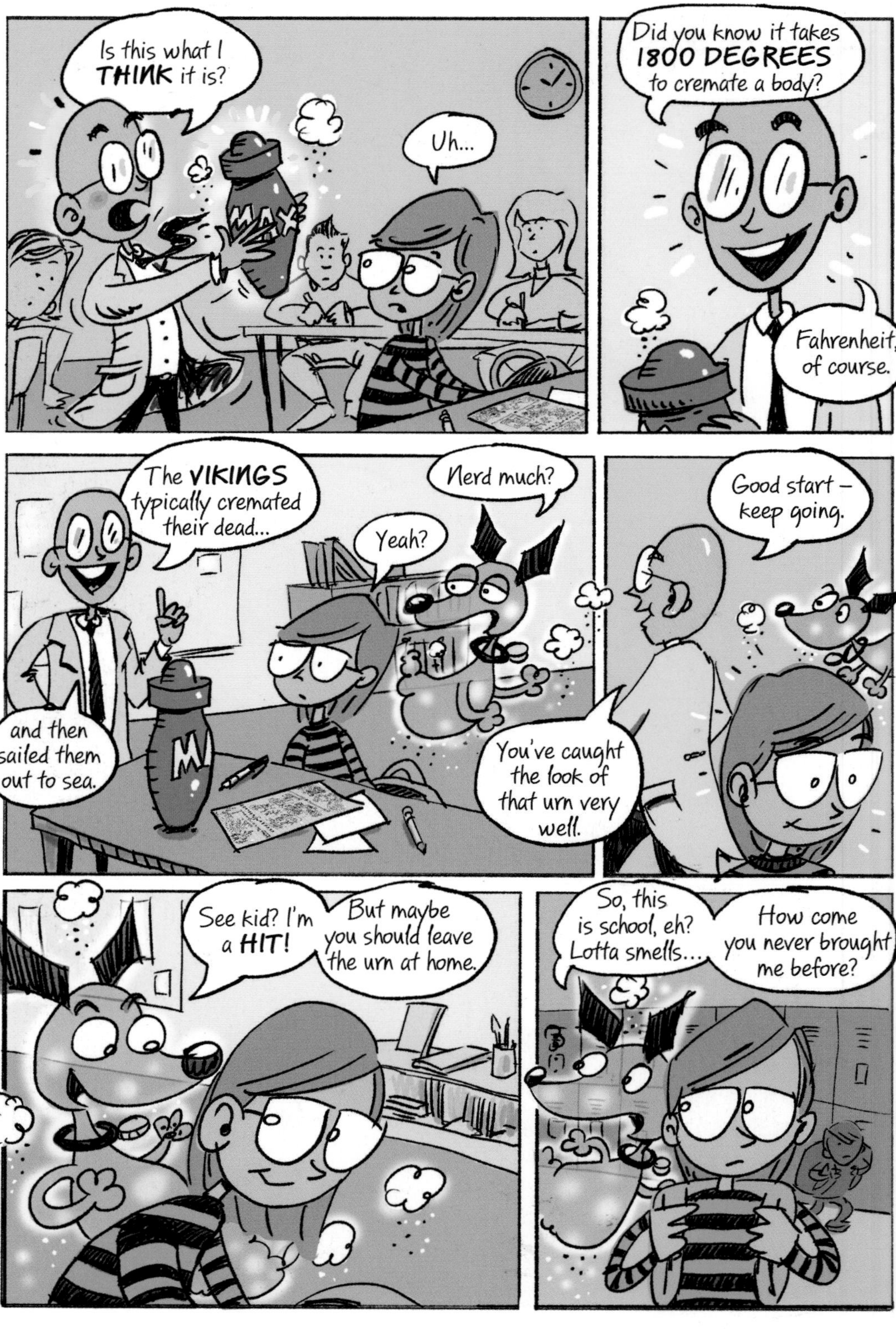

Is this what I **THINK** it is?
Uh...
Did you know it takes **1800 DEGREES** to cremate a body?
Fahrenheit, of course.
The **VIKINGS** typically cremated their dead...
and then sailed them out to sea.
Yeah?
Nerd much?
Good start – keep going.
You've caught the look of that urn very well.
See kid? I'm a **HIT!**
But maybe you should leave the urn at home.
So, this is school, eh? Lotta smells...
How come you never brought me before?

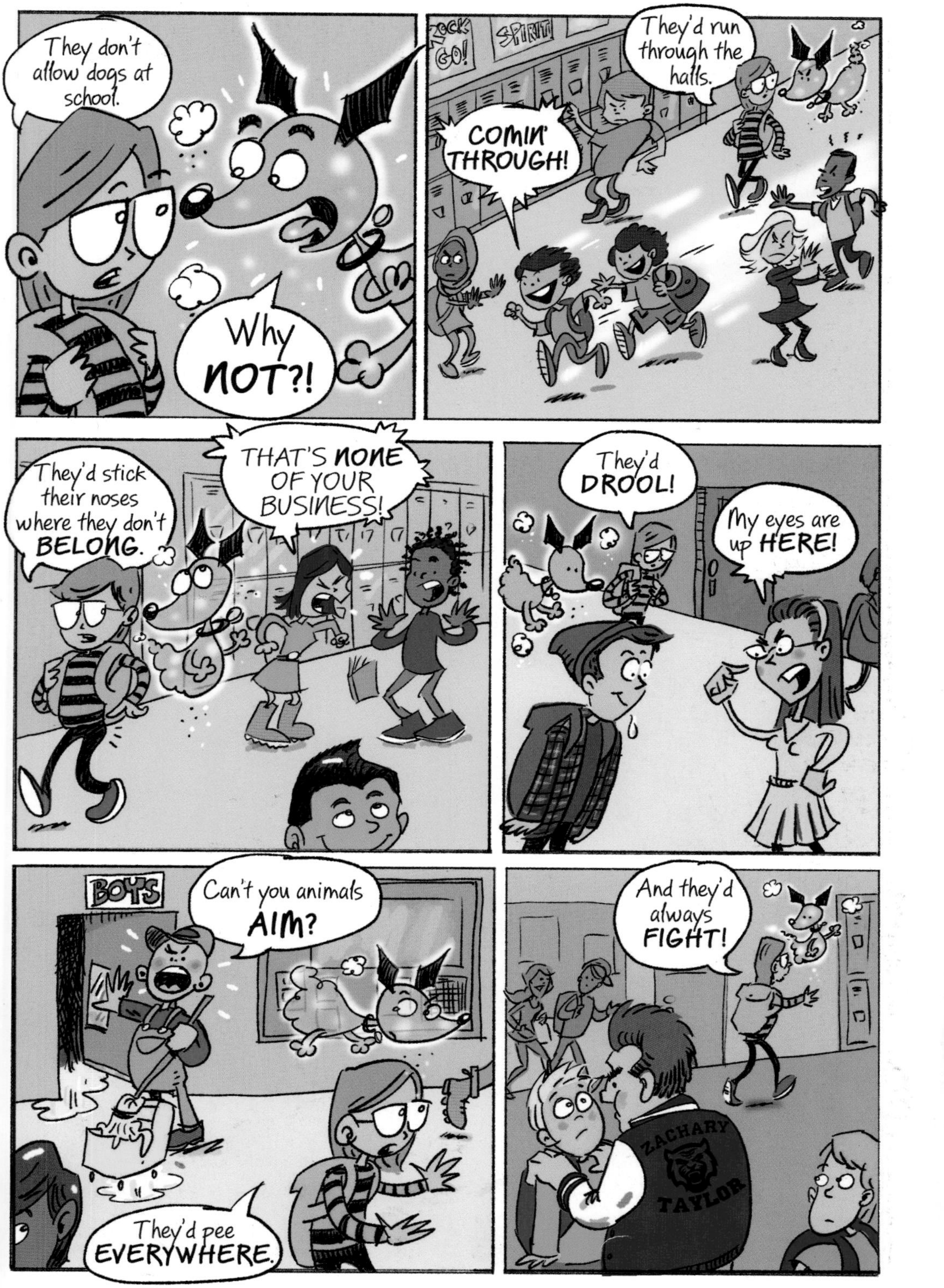
They don't allow dogs at school.
Why NOT?!
ROCK GO!
SPIRIT
They'd run through the halls.
COMIN' THROUGH!
They'd stick their noses where they don't BELONG.
THAT'S NONE OF YOUR BUSINESS!
They'd DROOL!
My eyes are up HERE!
BOYS
Can't you animals AIM?
They'd pee EVERYWHERE.
And they'd always FIGHT!
ZACHARY
TAYLOR

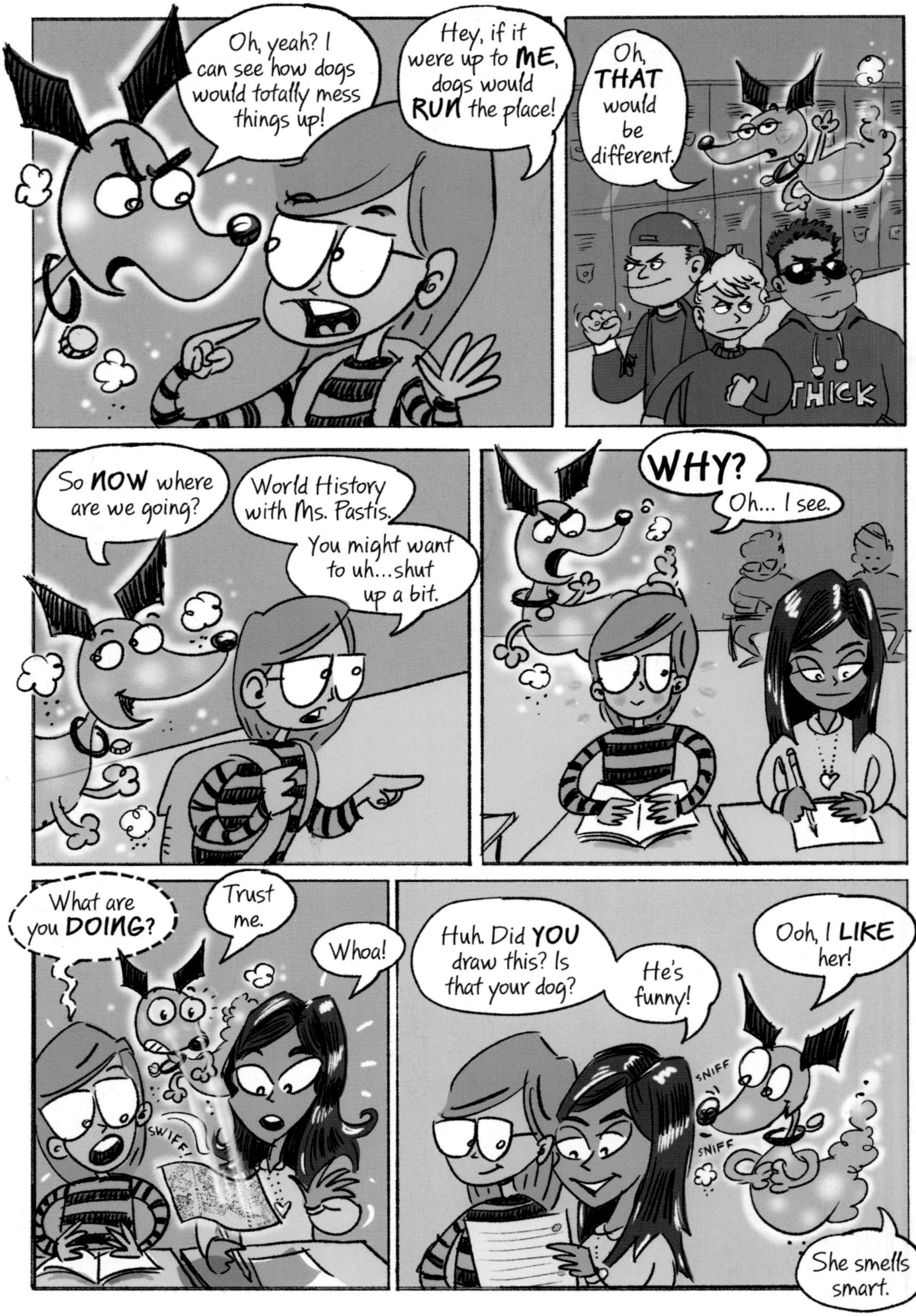
Oh, yeah? I can see how dogs would totally mess things up!
Hey, if it were up to **ME**, dogs would **RUN** the place!
Oh, **THAT** would be different.
THICK
So **NOW** where are we going?
World History with Ms. Pastis.
You might want to uh...shut up a bit.
WHY?
Oh... I see.
What are you **DOING?**
Trust me.
Whoa!
SWIFF
Huh. Did **YOU** draw this? Is that your dog?
He's funny!
Ooh, I **LIKE** her!
SNIFF
SNIFF
She smells smart.

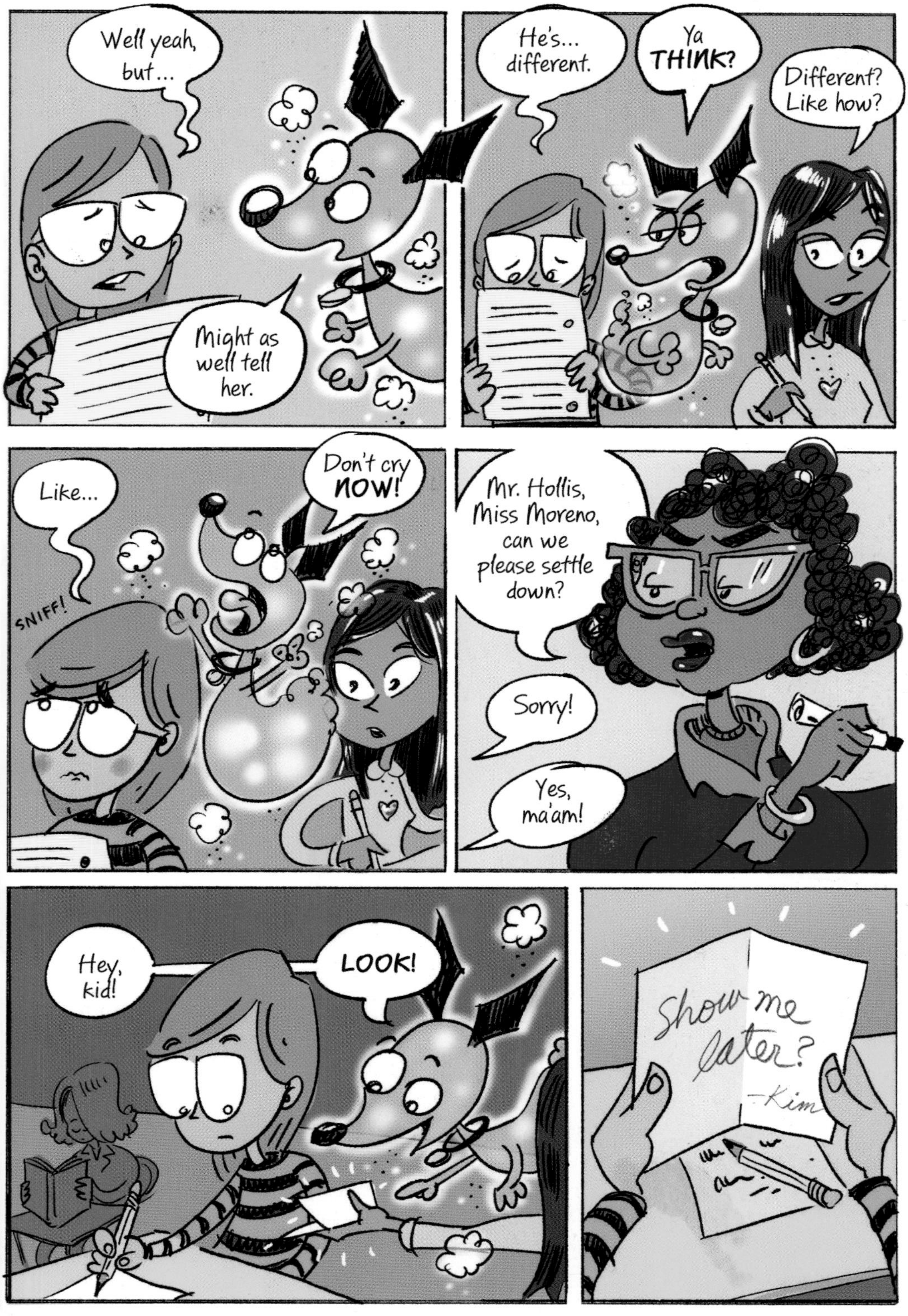

Well yeah, but...
Might as well tell her.
He's... different.
Ya THINK?
Different? Like how?
Like...
SNIFF!
Don't cry NOW!
Mr. Hollis, Miss Moreno, can we please settle down?
Sorry!
Yes, ma'am!
Hey, kid!
LOOK!
Show me later?
-Kim

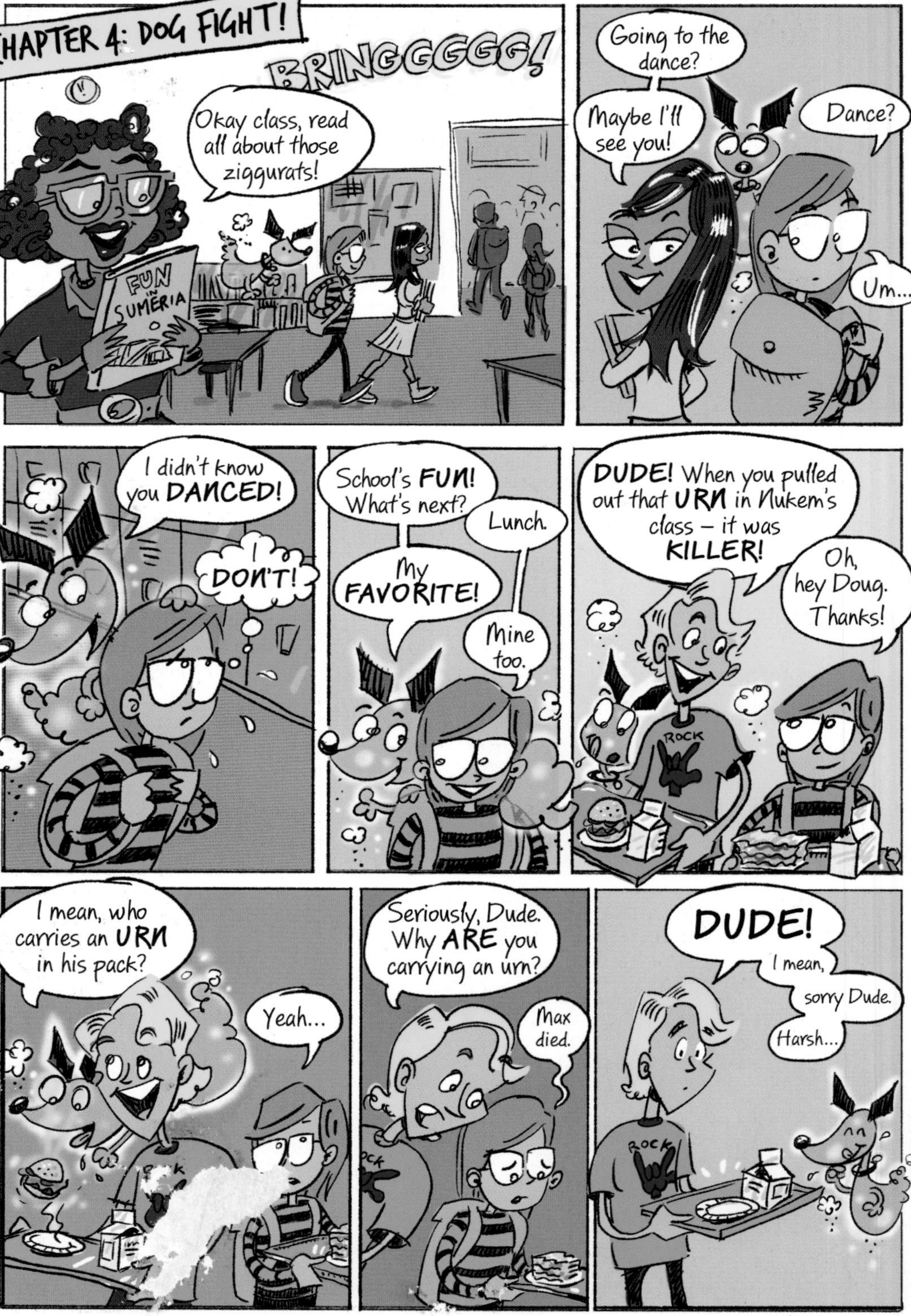
CHAPTER 4: DOG FIGHT!
BRINGGGGG!
Okay class, read all about those ziggurats!
FUN IN SUMERIA
Going to the dance?
Maybe I'll see you!
Dance?
Um...
I didn't know you DANCED!
I DON'T!
School's FUN! What's next?
Lunch.
My FAVORITE!
Mine too.
DUDE! When you pulled out that URN in Nukem's class – it was KILLER!
Oh, hey Doug. Thanks!
ROCK
I mean, who carries an URN in his pack?
Yeah...
Seriously, Dude. Why ARE you carrying an urn?
Max died.
DUDE!
I mean,
sorry Dude.
Harsh...

23

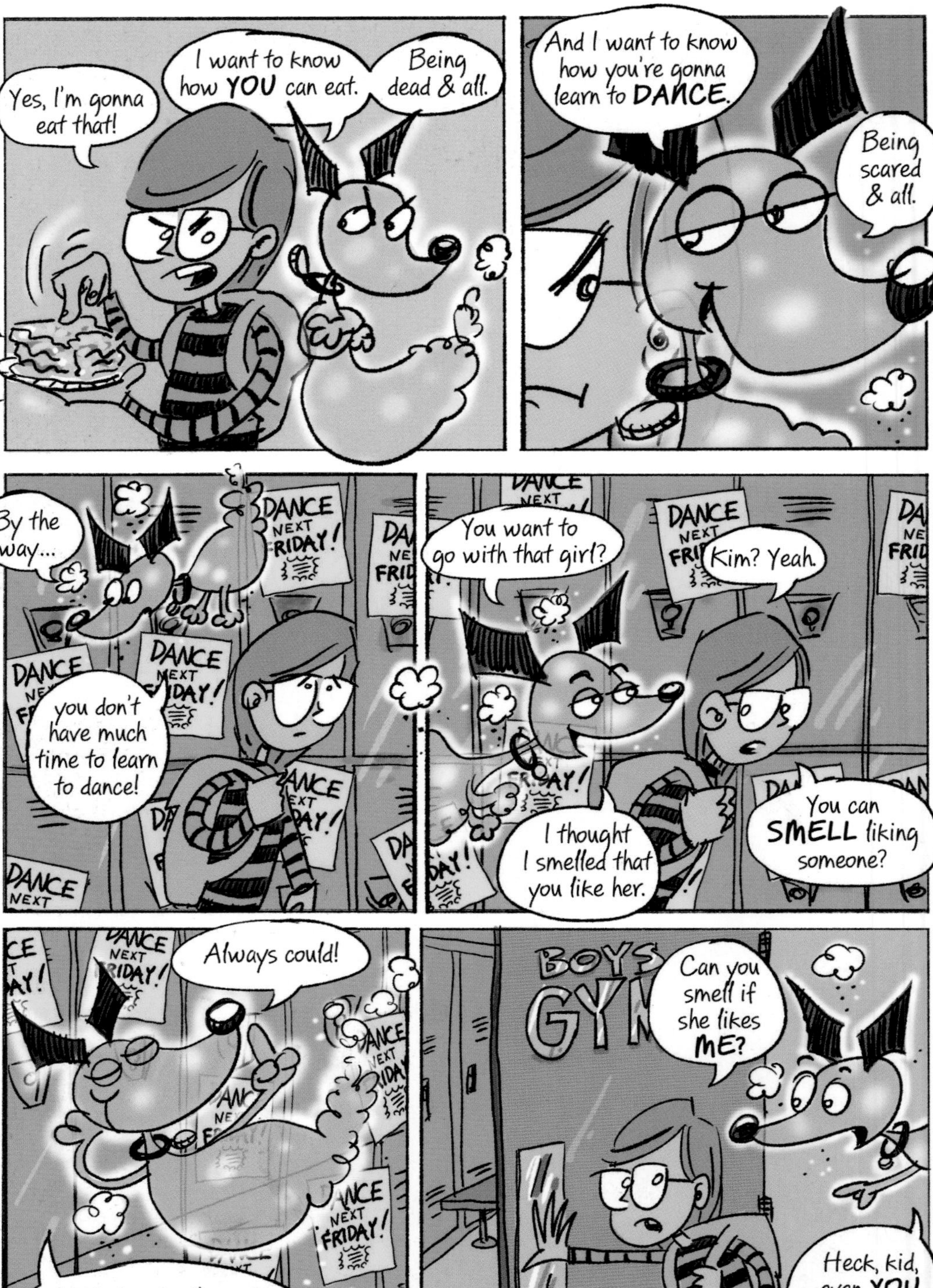
Yes, I'm gonna eat that!
I want to know how YOU can eat.
Being dead & all.
And I want to know how you're gonna learn to DANCE.
Being scared & all.
By the way...
you don't have much time to learn to dance!
DANCE NEXT FRIDAY!
You want to go with that girl?
Kim? Yeah.
I thought I smelled that you like her.
You can SMELL liking someone?
Always could!
And being dead's made my sniffer even BETTER!
BOYS GYM
Can you smell if she likes ME?
Heck, kid, even YOU can do that!

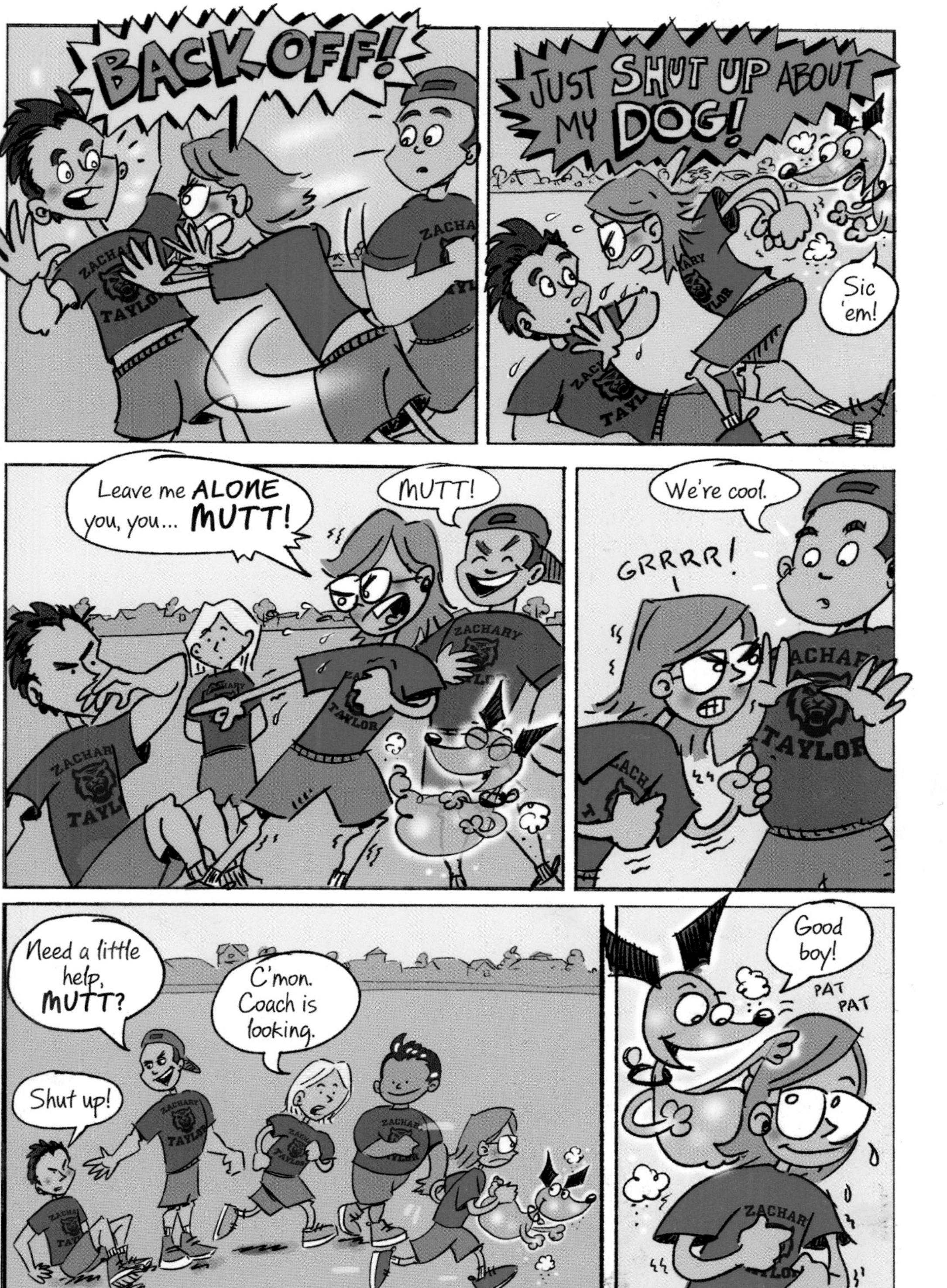
BACK OFF!
JUST SHUT UP ABOUT MY DOG!
Sic 'em!
Leave me ALONE you, you... MUTT!
MUTT!
We're cool.
GRRRR!
Need a little help, MUTT?
Shut up!
C'mon. Coach is looking.
Good boy!
PAT PAT

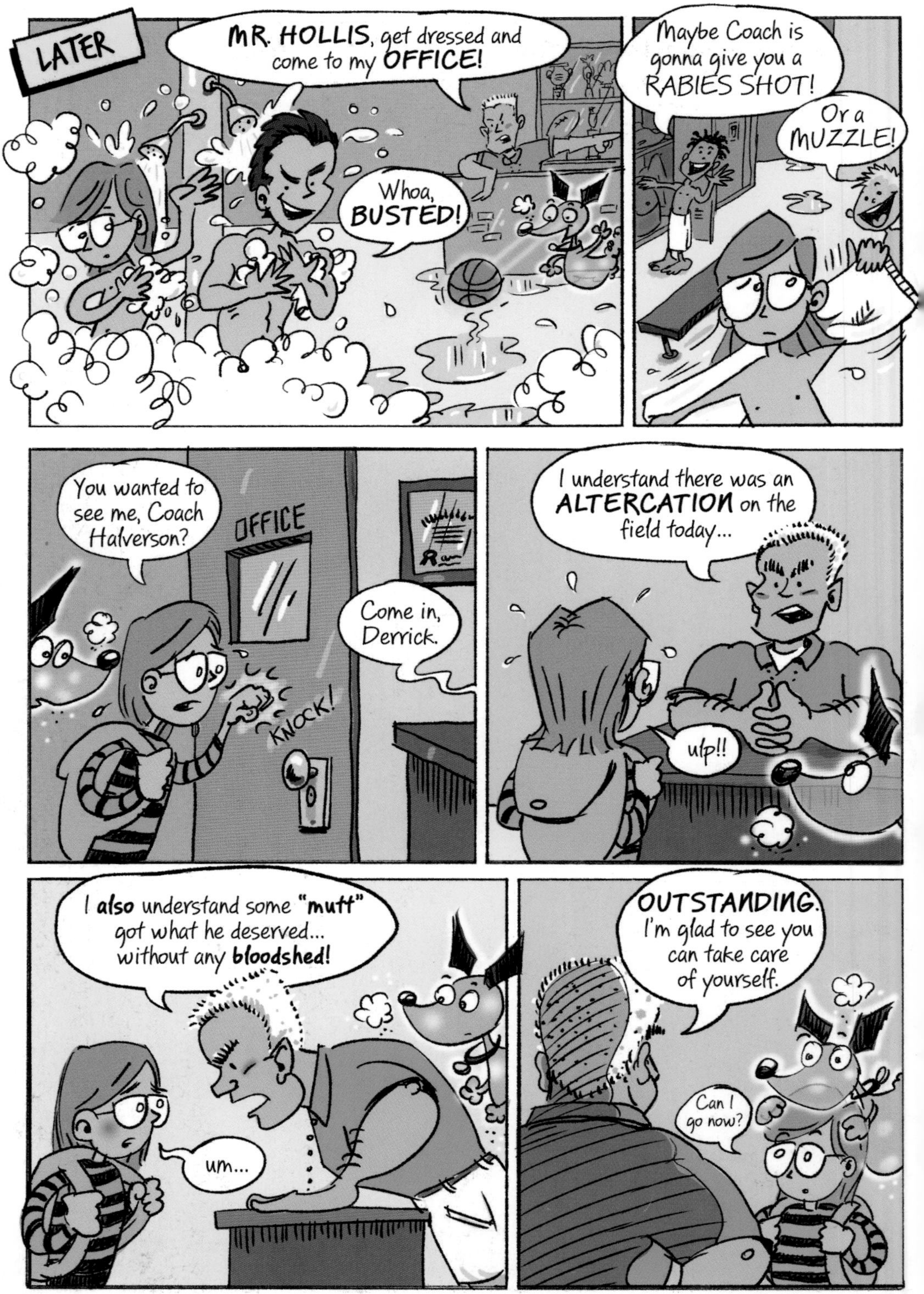
LATER
MR. HOLLIS, get dressed and come to my OFFICE!
Whoa, BUSTED!
Maybe Coach is gonna give you a RABIES SHOT!
Or a MUZZLE!
You wanted to see me, Coach Halverson?
OFFICE
KNOCK!
Come in, Derrick.
I understand there was an ALTERCATION on the field today...
ulp!!
I also understand some "mutt" got what he deserved... without any bloodshed!
um...
OUTSTANDING. I'm glad to see you can take care of yourself.
Can I go now?

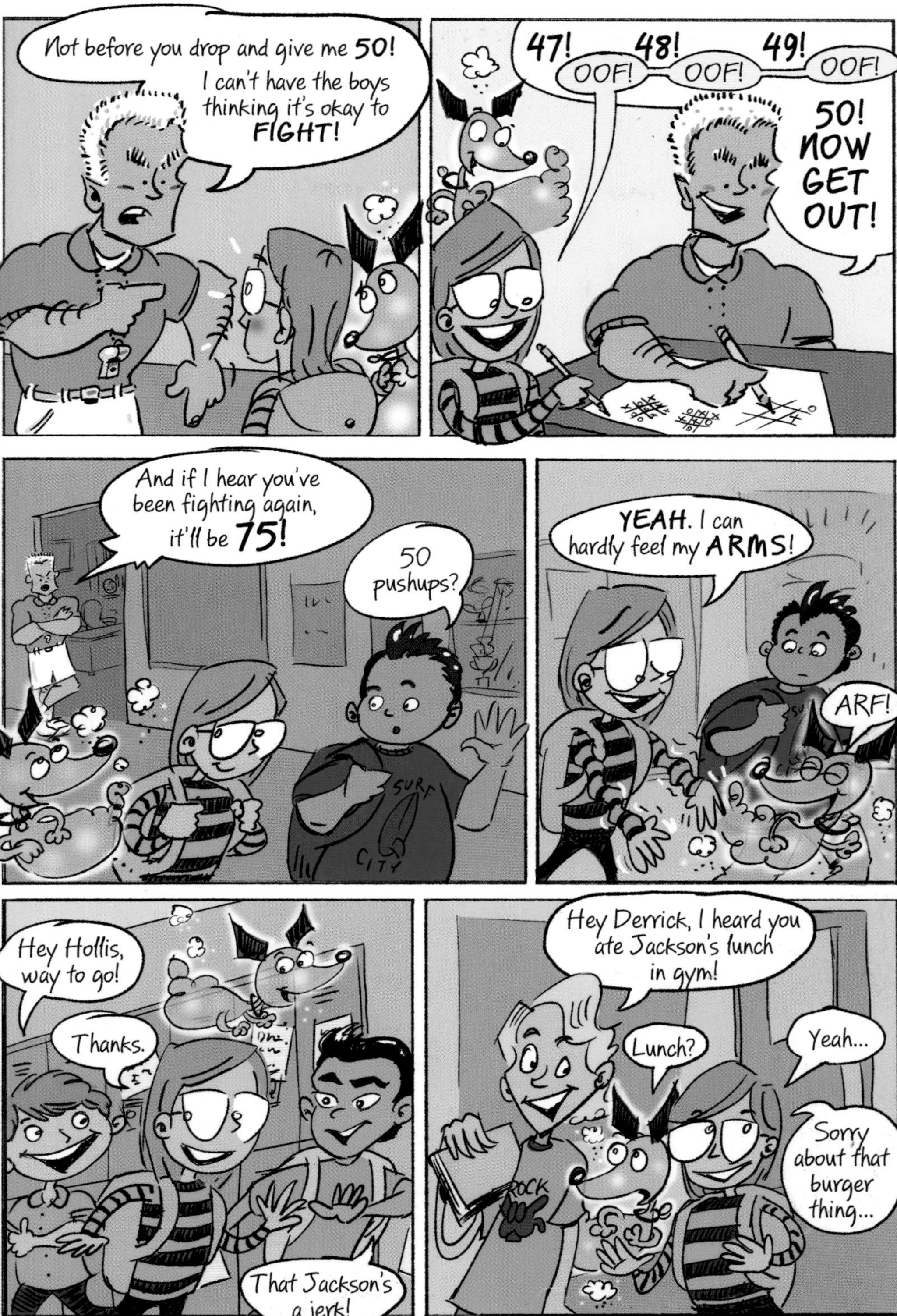

Not before you drop and give me 50!
I can't have the boys thinking it's okay to FIGHT!
47!
OOF!
48!
OOF!
49!
OOF!
50! NOW GET OUT!
And if I hear you've been fighting again, it'll be 75!
50 pushups?
SURF CITY
YEAH. I can hardly feel my ARMS!
ARF!
Hey Hollis, way to go!
Thanks.
That Jackson's a jerk!
Hey Derrick, I heard you ate Jackson's lunch in gym!
Lunch?
Yeah...
Sorry about that burger thing...
ROCK

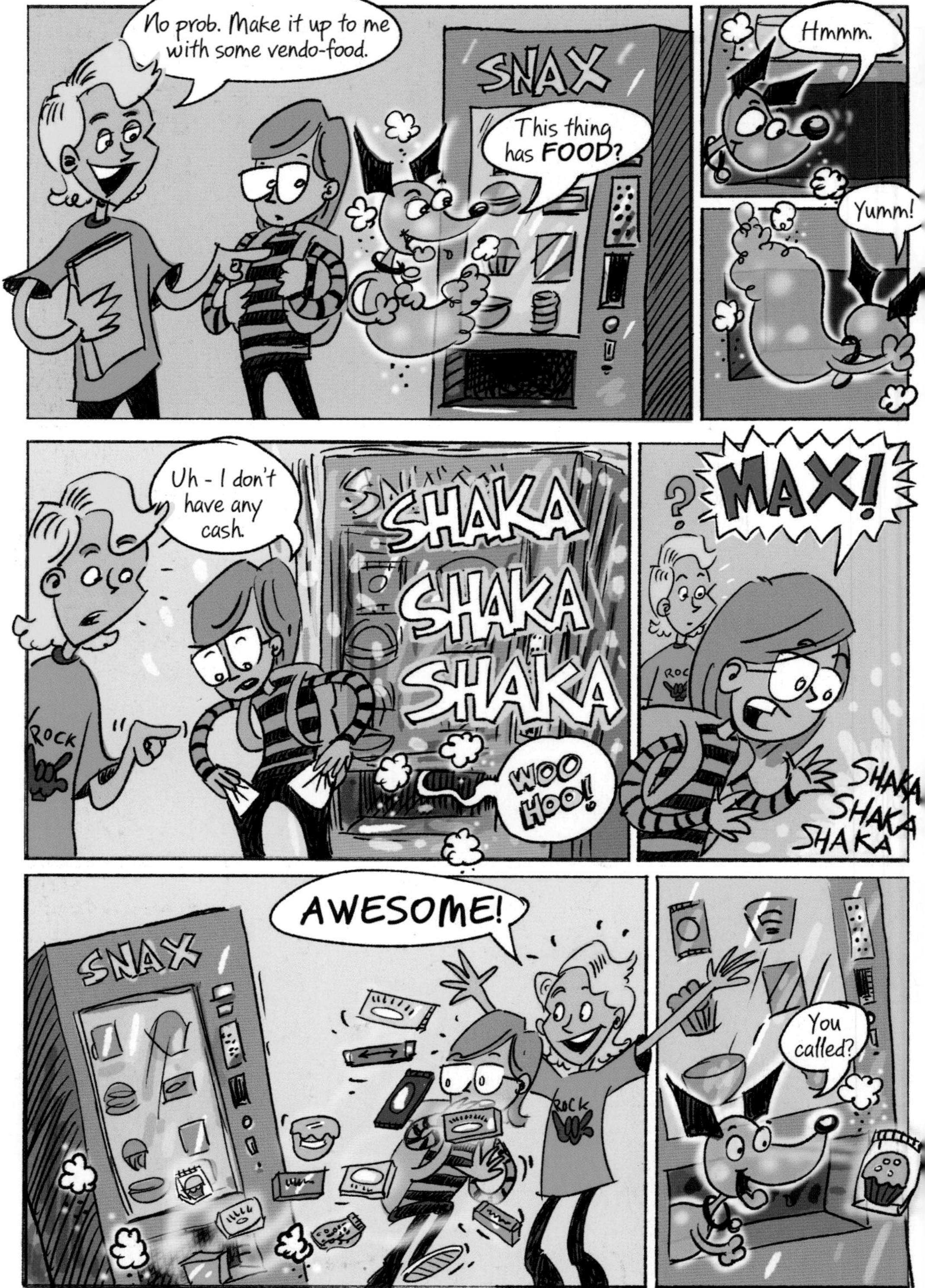
No prob. Make it up to me with some vendo-food.
SNAX
This thing has FOOD?
Hmmm.
Yumm!
Uh - I don't have any cash.
SHAKA SHAKA SHAKA
WOO HOO!
?
MAX!
SHAKA SHAKA SHAKA
AWESOME!
SNAX
You called?

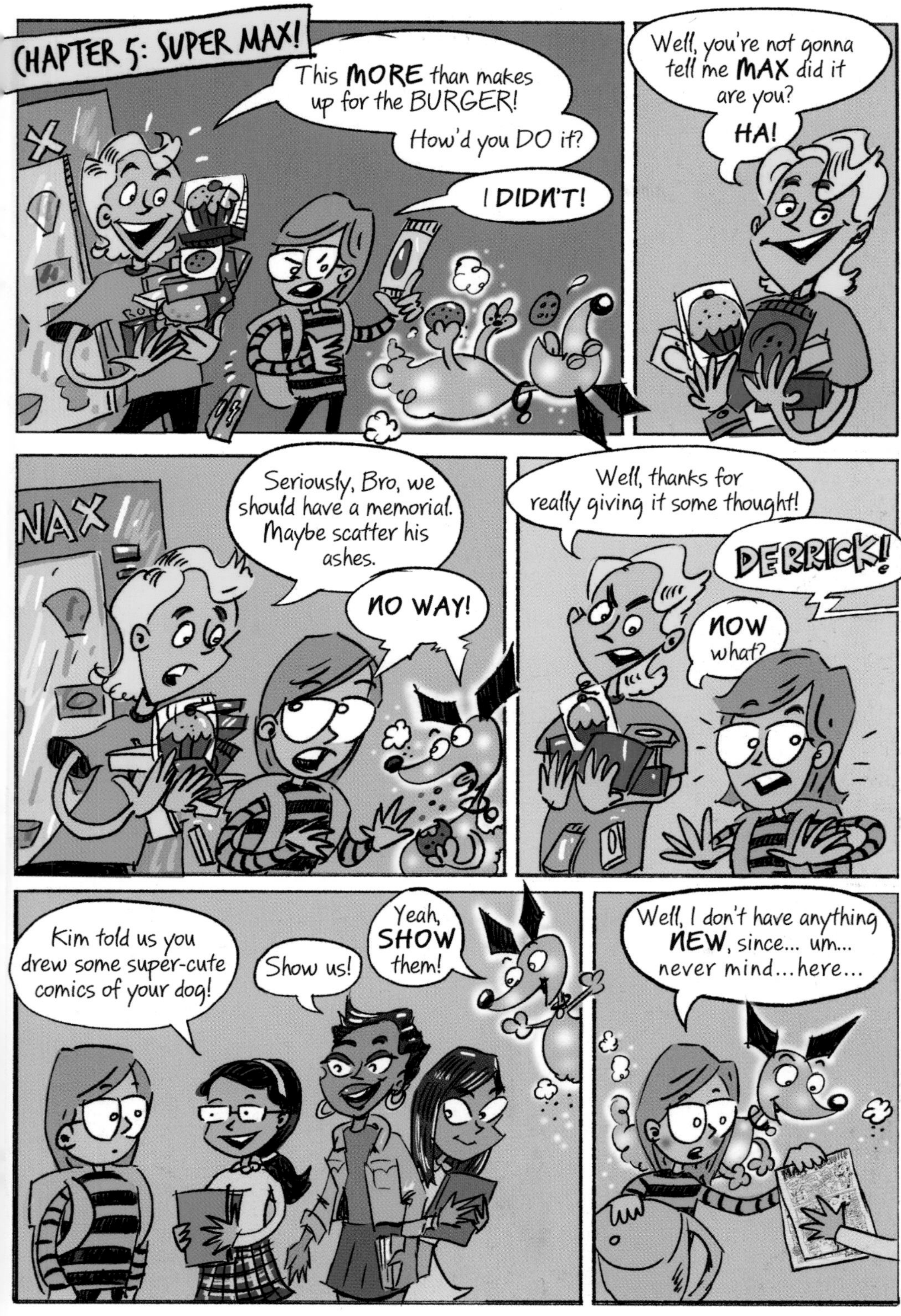
CHAPTER 5: SUPER MAX!
This MORE than makes up for the BURGER!
How'd you DO it?
I DIDN'T!
Well, you're not gonna tell me MAX did it are you?
HA!
Seriously, Bro, we should have a memorial. Maybe scatter his ashes.
NO WAY!
Well, thanks for really giving it some thought!
DERRICK!
NOW what?
Kim told us you drew some super-cute comics of your dog!
Show us!
Yeah, SHOW them!
Well, I don't have anything NEW, since... um... never mind...here...

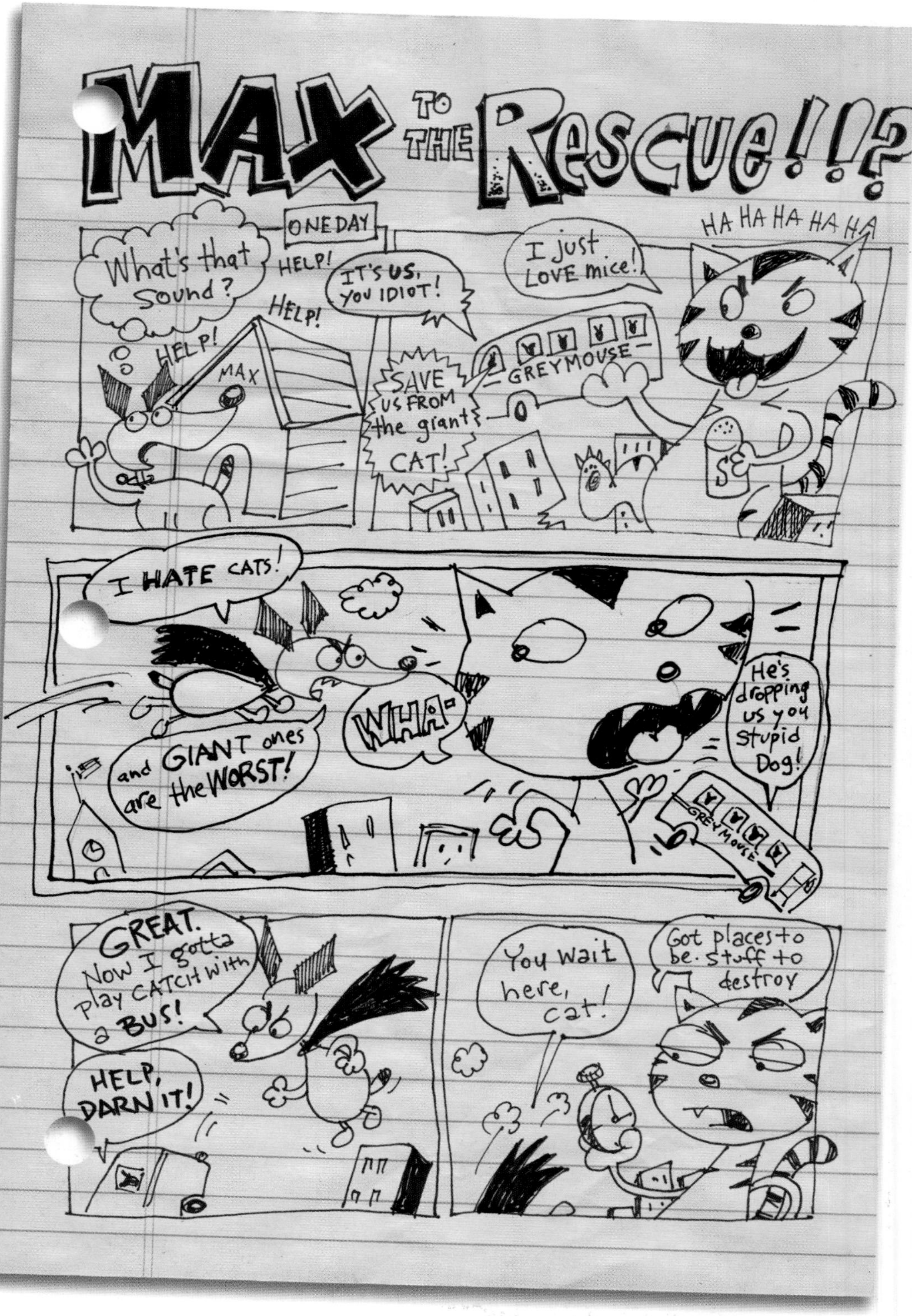
MAX TO THE RESCUE!!?
ONE DAY
What's that sound?
HELP!
HELP!
HELP!
MAX
IT'S US, YOU IDIOT!
SAVE US FROM the giant CAT!
GREYMOUSE
I just LOVE mice!
HA HA HA HA HA
I HATE CATS!
and GIANT ones are the WORST!
WHA-
He's dropping us you stupid Dog!
GREYMOUSE
GREAT. Now I gotta play CATCH with a BUS!
HELP, DARN IT!
You wait here, cat!
Got places to be. stuff to destroy

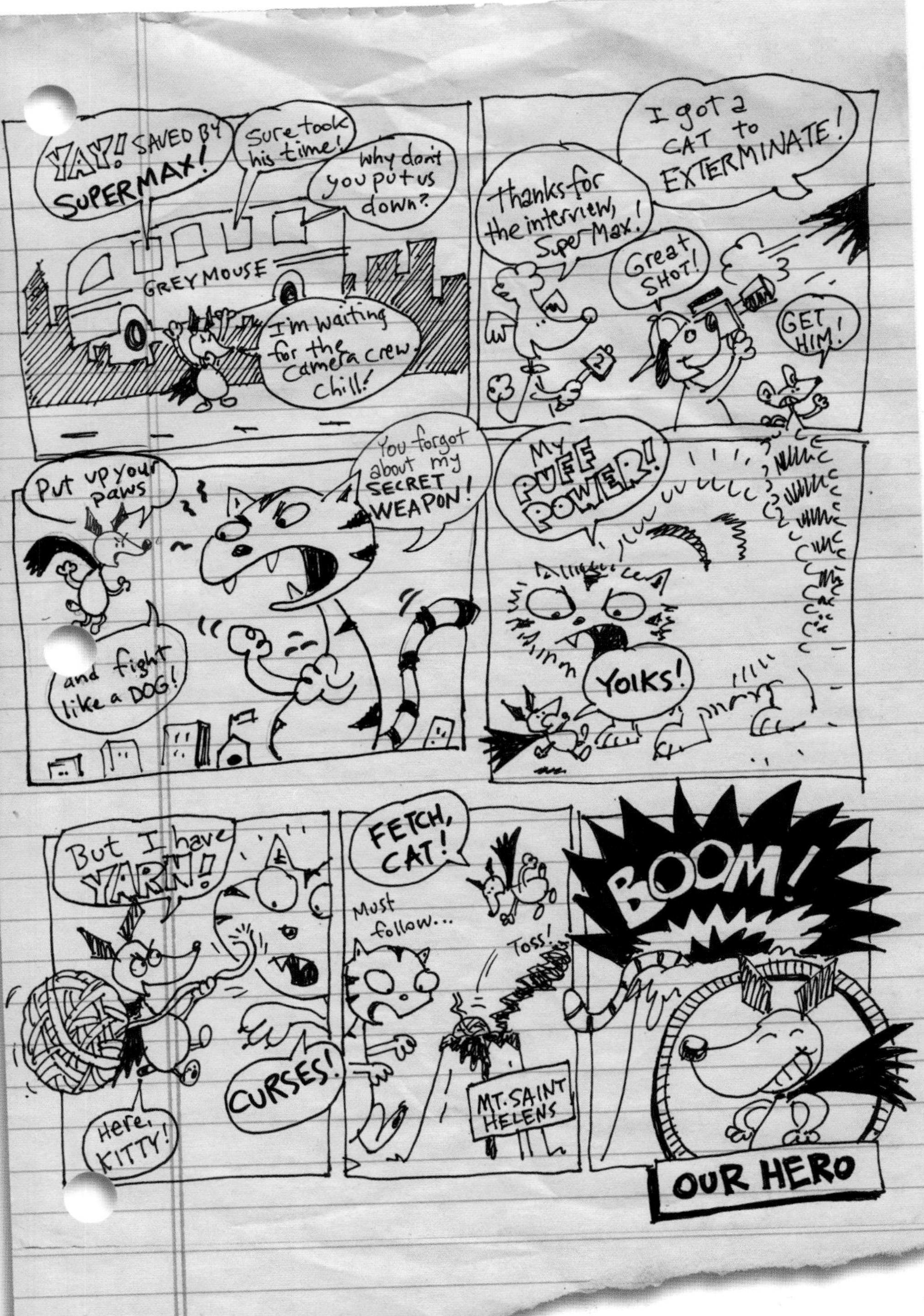

YAY! SAVED BY SUPERMAX!
Sure took his time!
Why don't you put us down?
GREYMOUSE
I'm waiting for the camera crew. Chill!
Thanks for the interview, SuperMax!
I got a CAT to EXTERMINATE!
Great SHOT!
GET HIM!
Put up your paws
and fight like a DOG!
You forgot about my SECRET WEAPON!
My PUFF POWER!
YOIKS!
But I have YARN!
Here, KITTY!
CURSES!
FETCH, CAT!
Must follow...
Toss!
MT. SAINT HELENS
BOOM!
OUR HERO

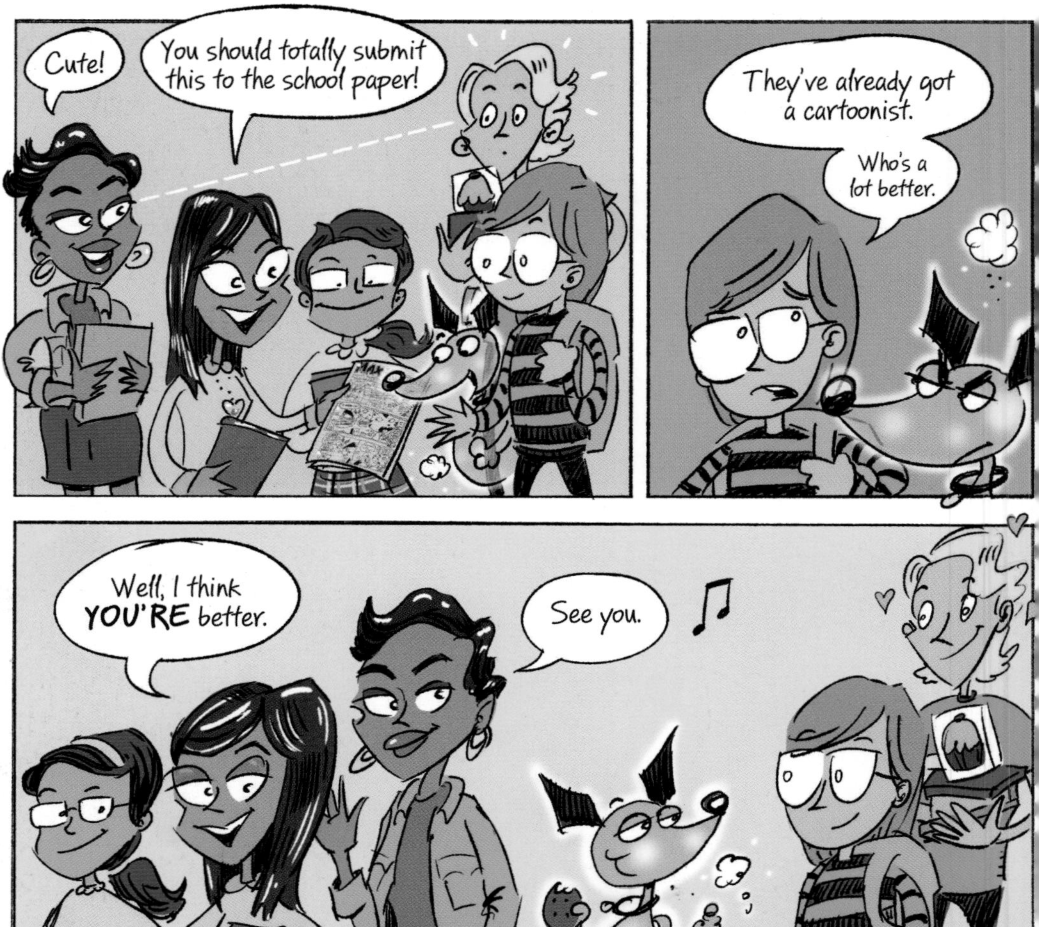
Cute!
You should totally submit this to the school paper!
They've already got a cartoonist.
Who's a lot better.
Well, I think **YOU'RE** better.
See you.
I think you have a real fan there!
SWIOOSH!
Hey, what's this one?
SNATCH!
NO!
That one's **PRIVATE!**

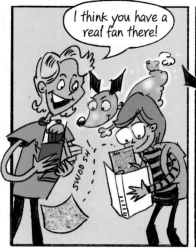

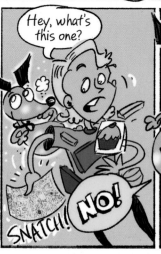

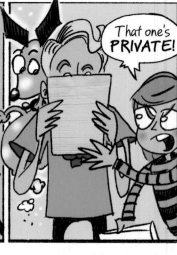

35

40

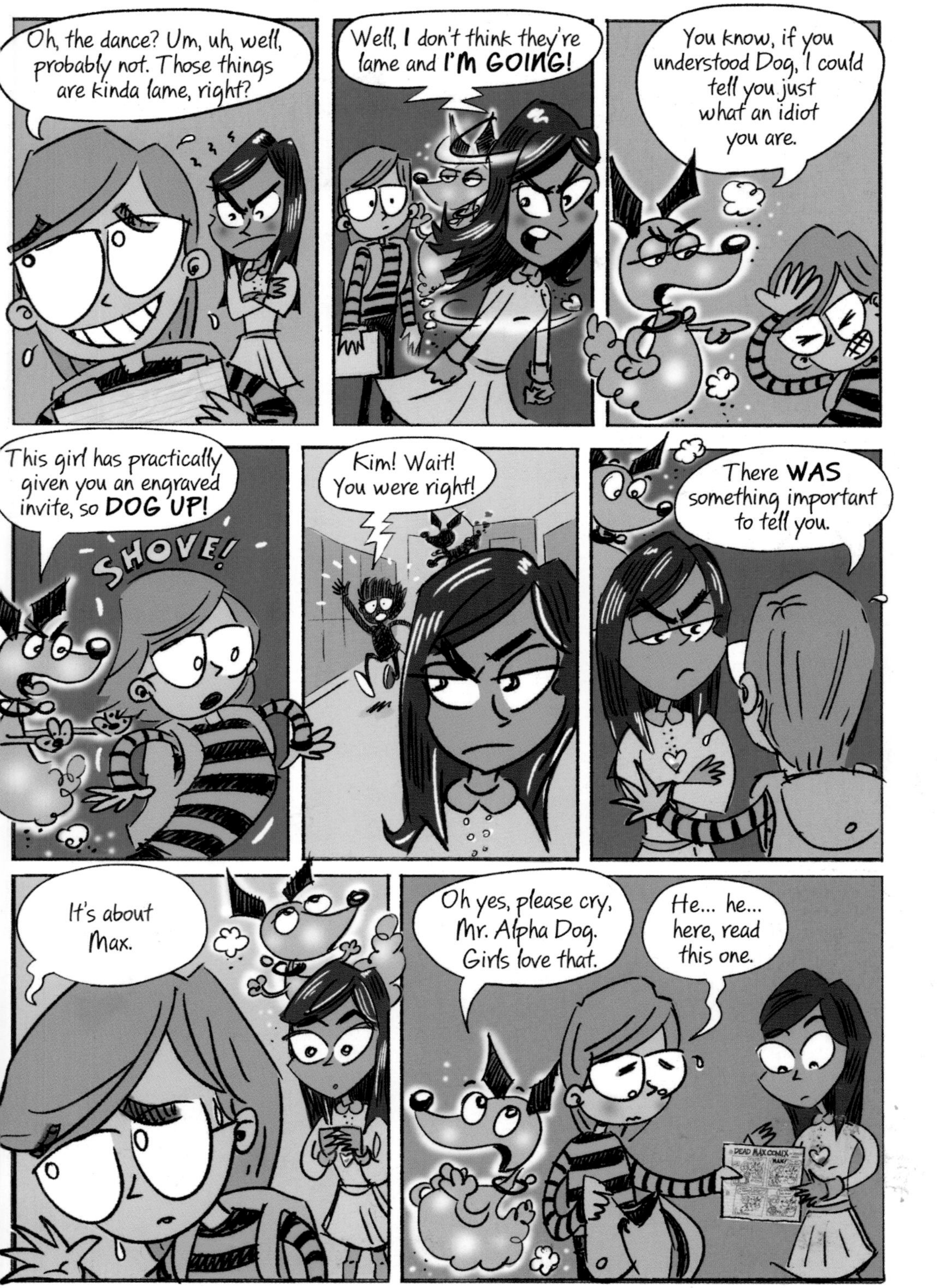

Oh, the dance? Um, uh, well, probably not. Those things are kinda lame, right?
Well, I don't think they're lame and I'M GOING!
You know, if you understood Dog, I could tell you just what an idiot you are.
This girl has practically given you an engraved invite, so DOG UP!
SHOVE!
Kim! Wait! You were right!
There WAS something important to tell you.
It's about Max.
Oh yes, please cry, Mr. Alpha Dog. Girls love that.
He... he... here, read this one.
DEAD MAX COMIX

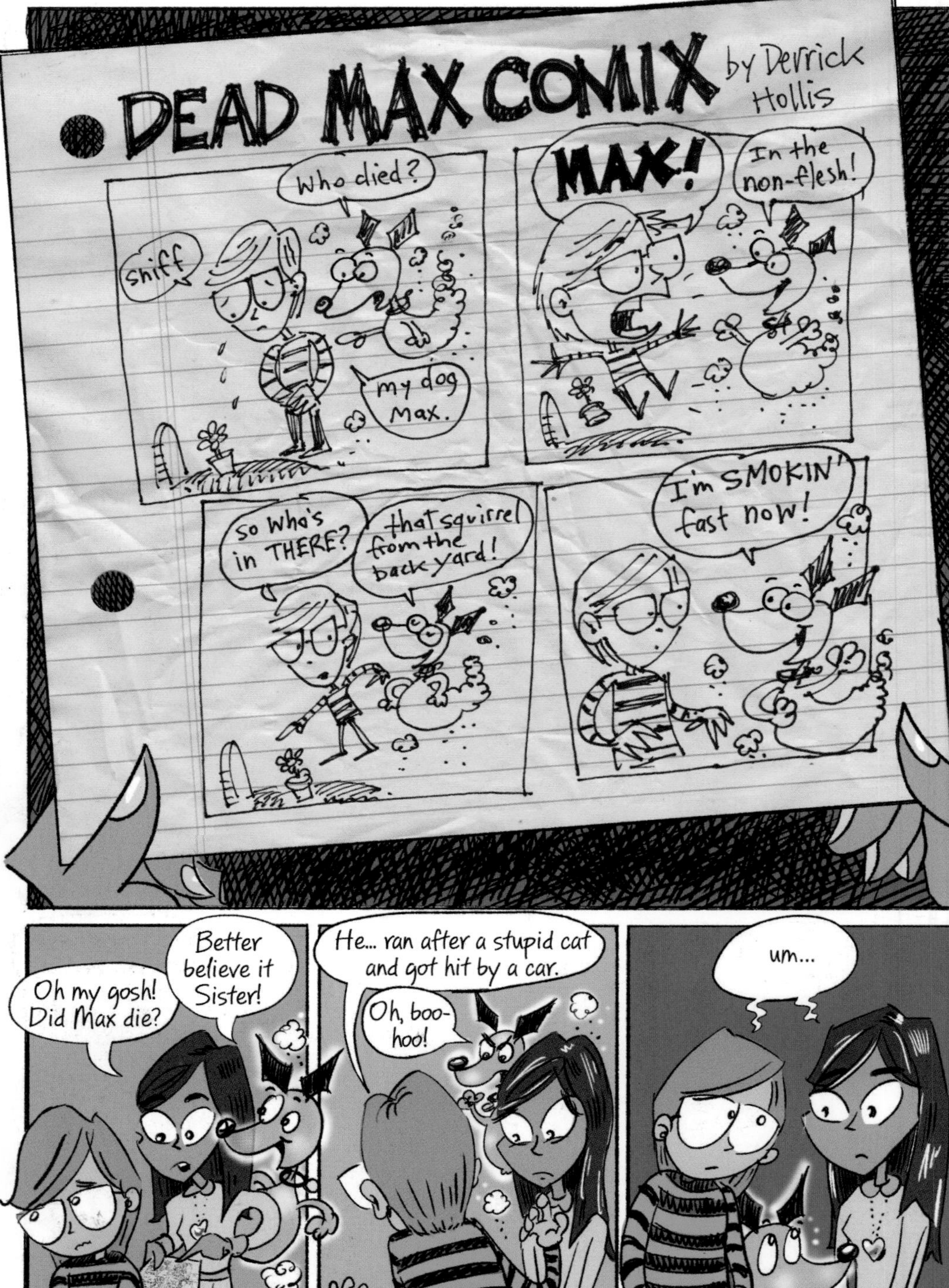
DEAD MAX COMIX
by Derrick Hollis
shiff
Who died?
my dog Max.
MAX!
In the non-flesh!
so Who's in THERE?
that squirrel from the back yard!
I'm SMOKIN' fast now!
Oh my gosh! Did Max die?
Better believe it Sister!
He... ran after a stupid cat and got hit by a car.
Oh, boo-hoo!
um...

Well, it's a really great comic. And it should be in the paper!

I mean, it's sad... But then it's funny!

And you should submit it.

Unless you're too chicken!

BAWK! BAWK!

I believe Max would like it. And he'd also tell you to ask a girl to the dance!

Let me know if you change your mind!

I do **NOT** get what she sees in you.

LATER

Hey, Sis, you know anything about um, dancing?

This doesn't have anything to do with your school dance, does it?

Wha-? No! What? Uh...

She's always been the smart one of the litter!

Here's your first lesson: ask the lady to dance.

44

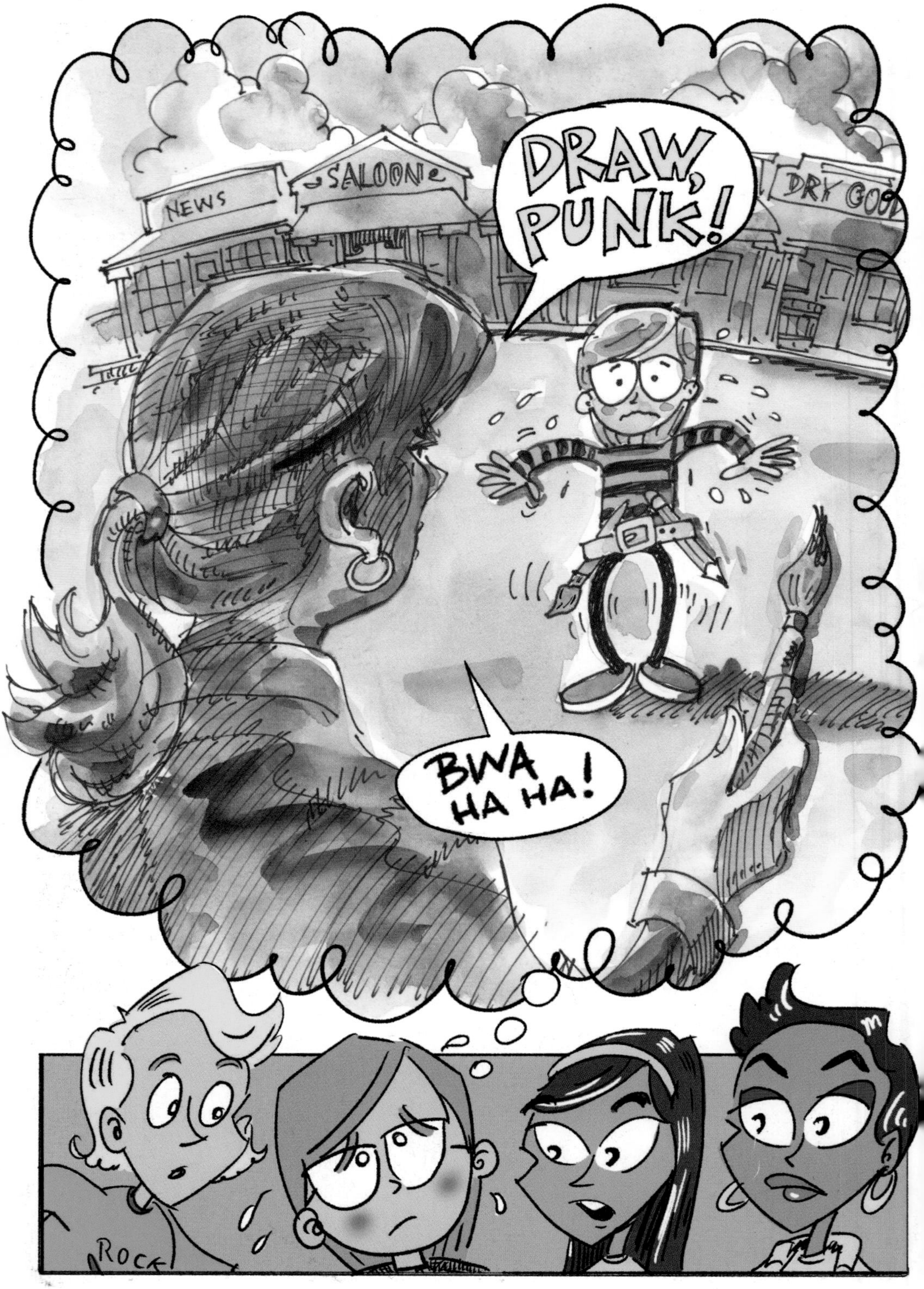
NEWS
SALOON
DRY GOOD
DRAW, PUNK!
BWA HA HA!
ROCK

47

48

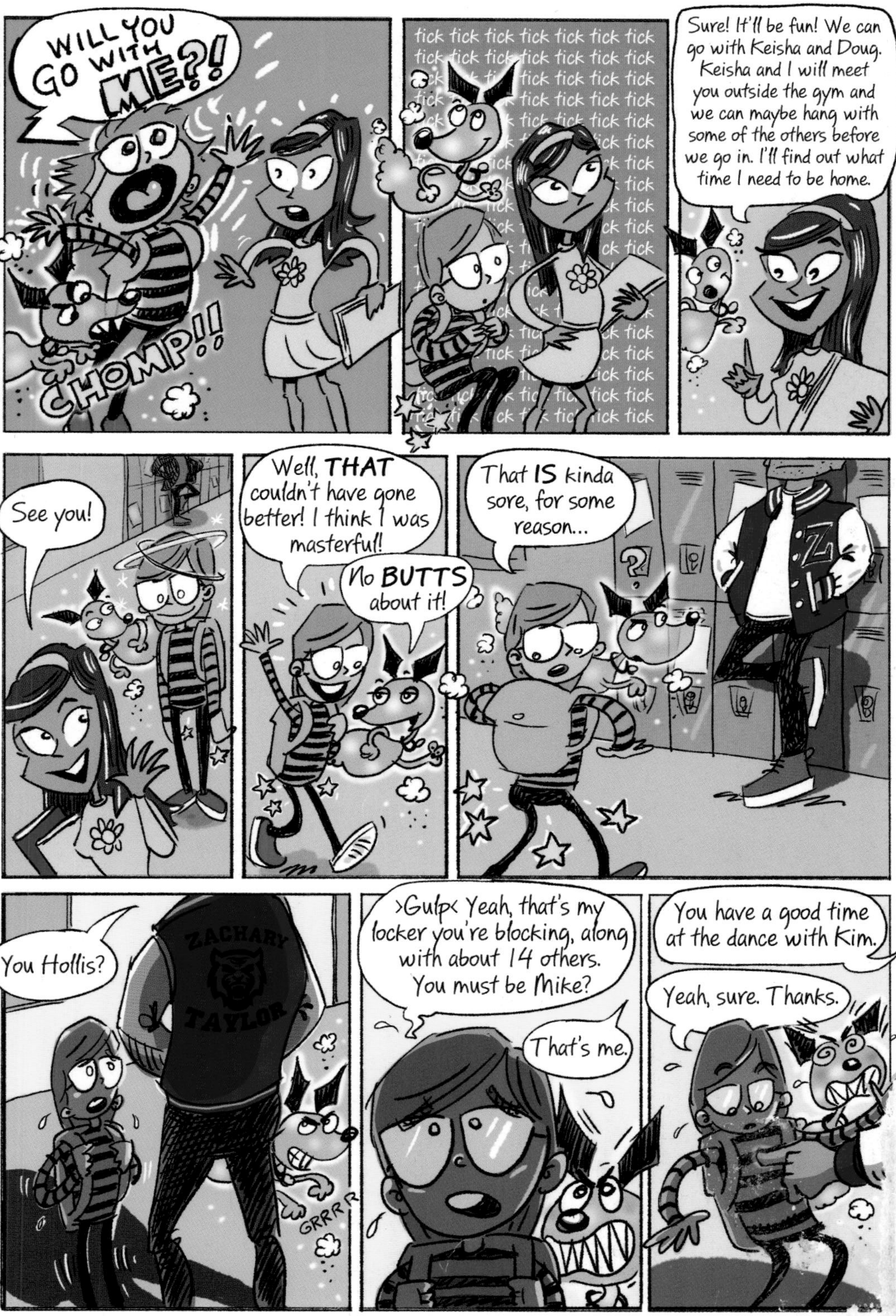
WILL YOU GO WITH ME?!
CHOMP!!
tick tick tick tick tick tick tick
Sure! It'll be fun! We can go with Keisha and Doug. Keisha and I will meet you outside the gym and we can maybe hang with some of the others before we go in. I'll find out what time I need to be home.
See you!
Well, THAT couldn't have gone better! I think I was masterful!
No BUTTS about it!
That IS kinda sore, for some reason...
You Hollis?
ZACHARY TAYLOR
GRRRR
>Gulp< Yeah, that's my locker you're blocking, along with about 14 others. You must be Mike?
That's me.
You have a good time at the dance with Kim.
Yeah, sure. Thanks.

I think we were just given a message.

Luckily, we're too dense to get it!

Yeah! We have a dance to get ready for!

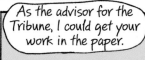

GRAPHIC ARTS

Mr. Hollis. I believe you have talent.

As the advisor for the Tribune, I could get your work in the paper.

Do you need new glasses? Can't you see what's in front of your face? Kim? The paper? If you never want anyone to see your work, you're on the right track!

Oh, no thanks, sir!

Or are you just a big CHICKEN?

SCRIBBLE
SCRIBBLE
SCRIBBLE

SUPER MAX vs the GIANT CHICKEN

WHOA! that's a BIG EGG!

RUN!

WHOOSH!

CRACK!

OW!

AT LAST! Free from that cursed SHELL!

He breathes FIRE?

I'm a SHE!

And I'm gonna sit on YOU!

Oh-woe is me!

No FAIR, you, you BIG CHICKEN!

WHAT THE SHELL? IS THIS THE END OF SUPER MAX?

TO BE CONTINUED

What's this?

SNATCH!

SWISH!

SNIC SNIC SNIC

BAHAHAHAHAH

I don't think anybody's ever seen him laugh before.

Ahem! Remember your comics are due tomorrow!

Oh, good. Back to normal.

No exceptions!

C'mon! Kim's got babaganoush for lunch!

Babaga-what?

Want some babaganoush?

Told you!

Our comics are due tomorrow.

And then the dance!

Yep. Of course, Mr. Teacher's Pet here is finished already.

SHOW! SHOW! SHOW! SHOW!
SHOW! SHOW! SHOW! SHOW!
SHOW! SHOW! SHOW! SHOW!
SHOW! SHOW! SHOW! SHOW!

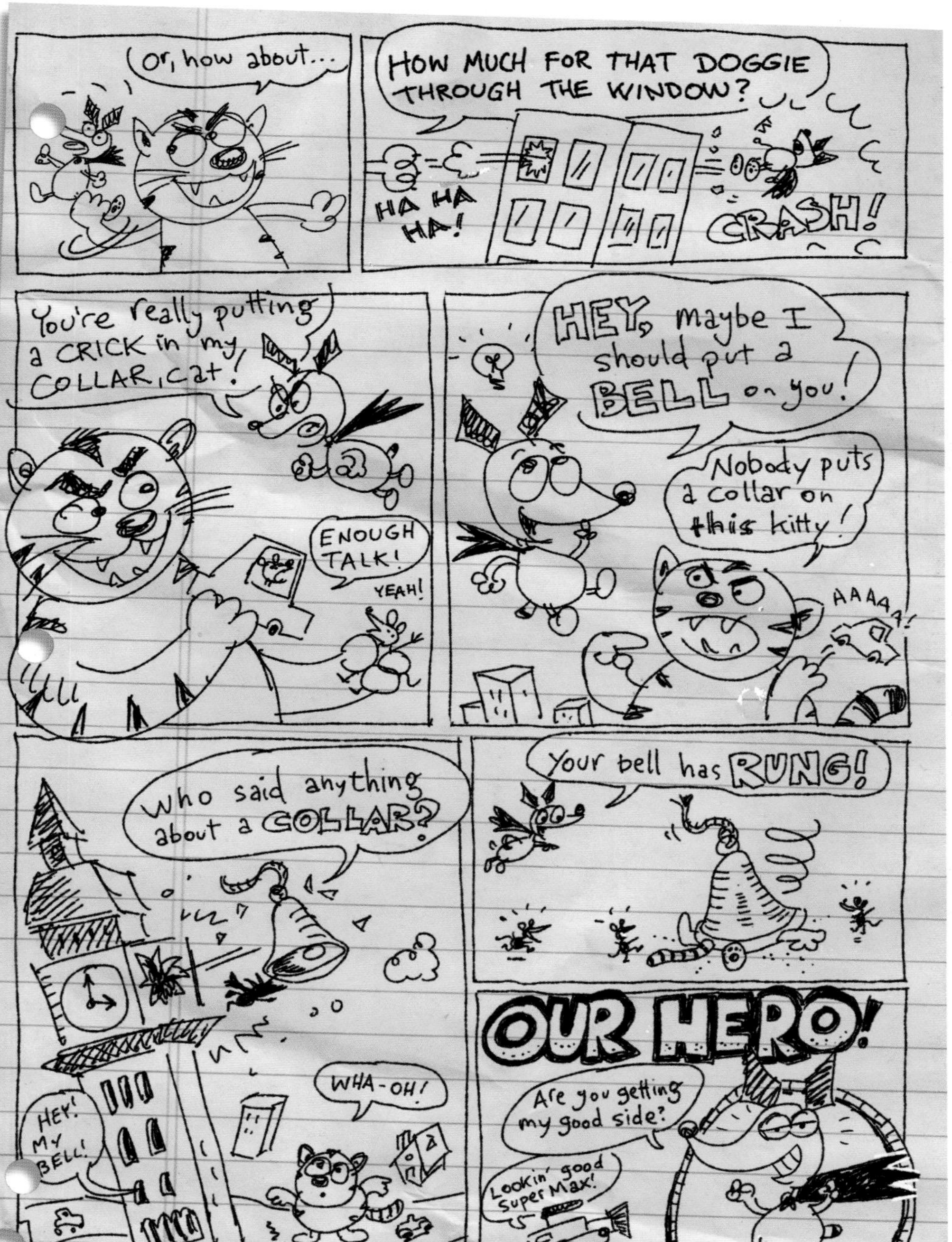

Or, how about...
HOW MUCH FOR THAT DOGGIE THROUGH THE WINDOW?
HA HA HA!
CRASH!
You're really putting a CRICK in my COLLAR, cat!
ENOUGH TALK!
YEAH!
HEY, maybe I should put a BELL on you!
Nobody puts a collar on this kitty!
AAAAA!
Who said anything about a COLLAR?
HEY! MY BELL!
WHA-OH!
Your bell has RUNG!
OUR HERO!
Are you getting my good side?
Lookin' good Super Max!
SUPER MAX!

It's wonderful!

So's this babaganoush!

C'mon, Super Artist, you gotta help me finish my comic!

And fix some snacks!

FRIDAY

Class, your comics are impressive!

But one is missing!

Dude, I totally saw your finished comic yesterday!

It's ruined.

I didn't finish...

Ruined?

Tell him who really ruined it.

My mom accidentally spilled some ink... and wine.

"Accidentally!"

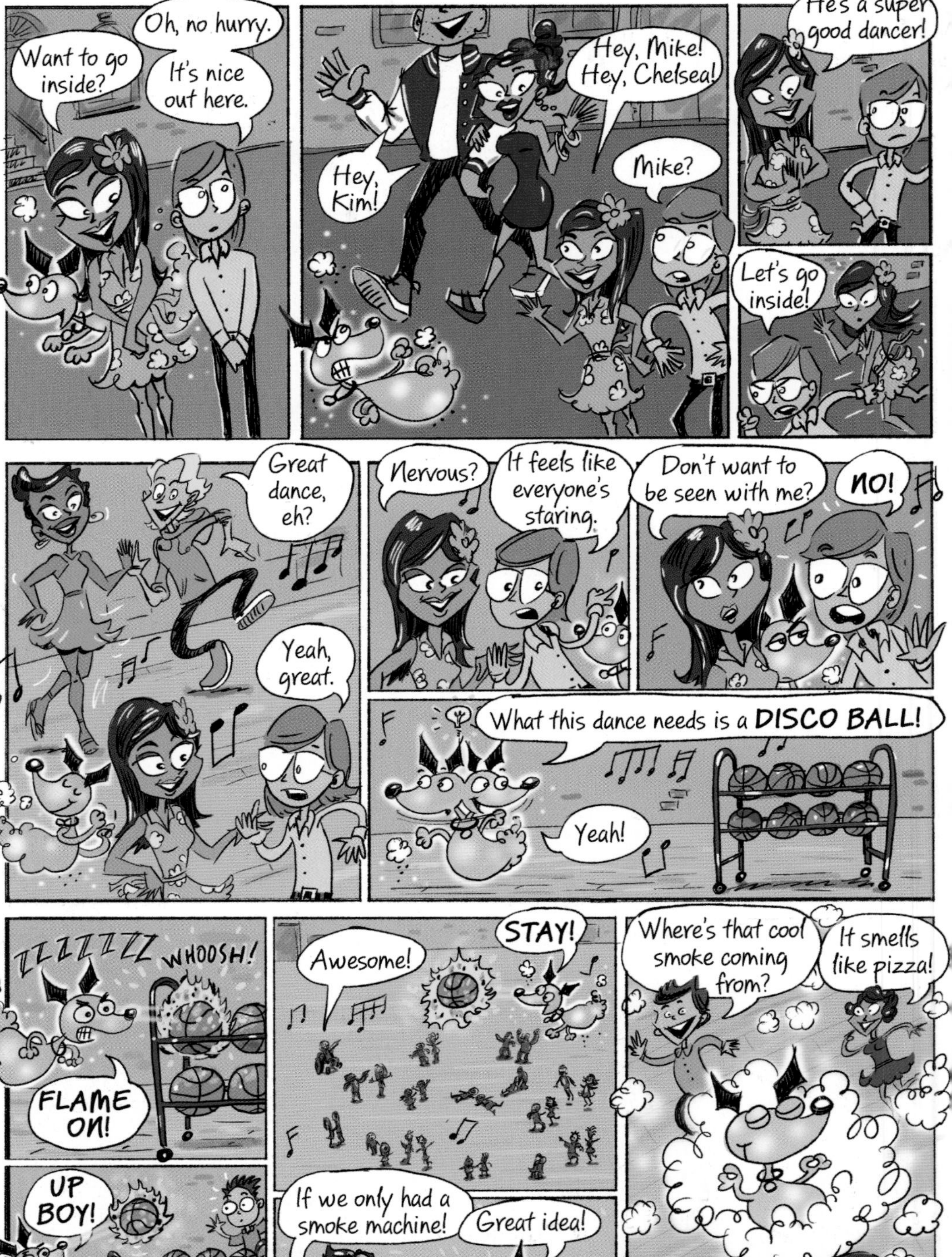
Want to go inside?
Oh, no hurry.
It's nice out here.
Hey, Mike! Hey, Chelsea!
Hey, Kim!
Mike?
He's a super good dancer!
Let's go inside!
Great dance, eh?
Yeah, great.
Nervous?
It feels like everyone's staring.
Don't want to be seen with me?
NO!
What this dance needs is a DISCO BALL!
Yeah!
ZZZZZZZ
WHOOSH!
FLAME ON!
UP BOY!
Awesome!
STAY!
If we only had a smoke machine!
Great idea!
Where's that cool smoke coming from?
It smells like pizza!

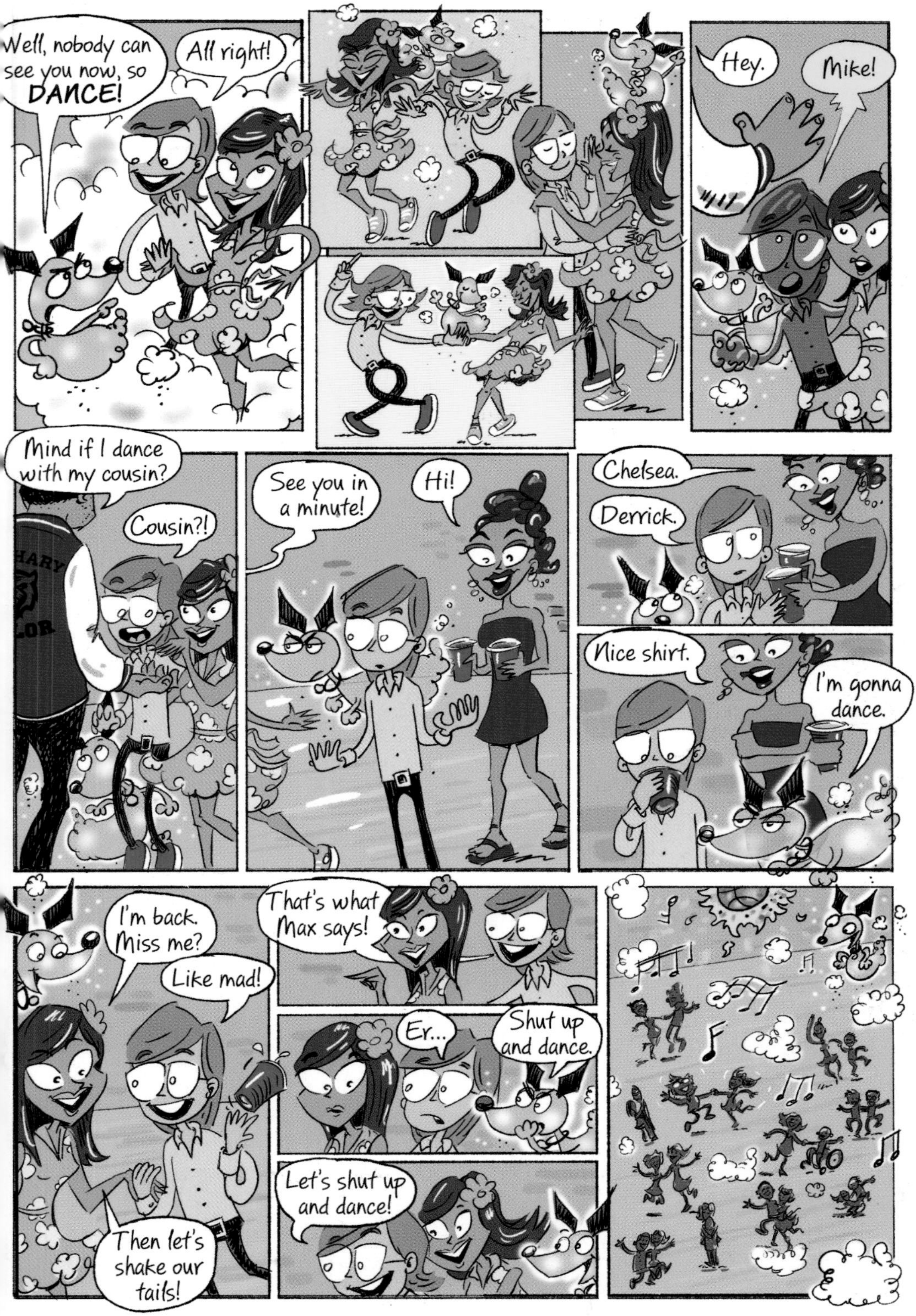

Well, nobody can see you now, so DANCE!
All right!
Hey.
Mike!
Mind if I dance with my cousin?
Cousin?!
See you in a minute!
Hi!
Chelsea.
Derrick.
Nice shirt.
I'm gonna dance.
I'm back. Miss me?
Like mad!
Then let's shake our tails!
That's what Max says!
Er...
Shut up and dance.
Let's shut up and dance!

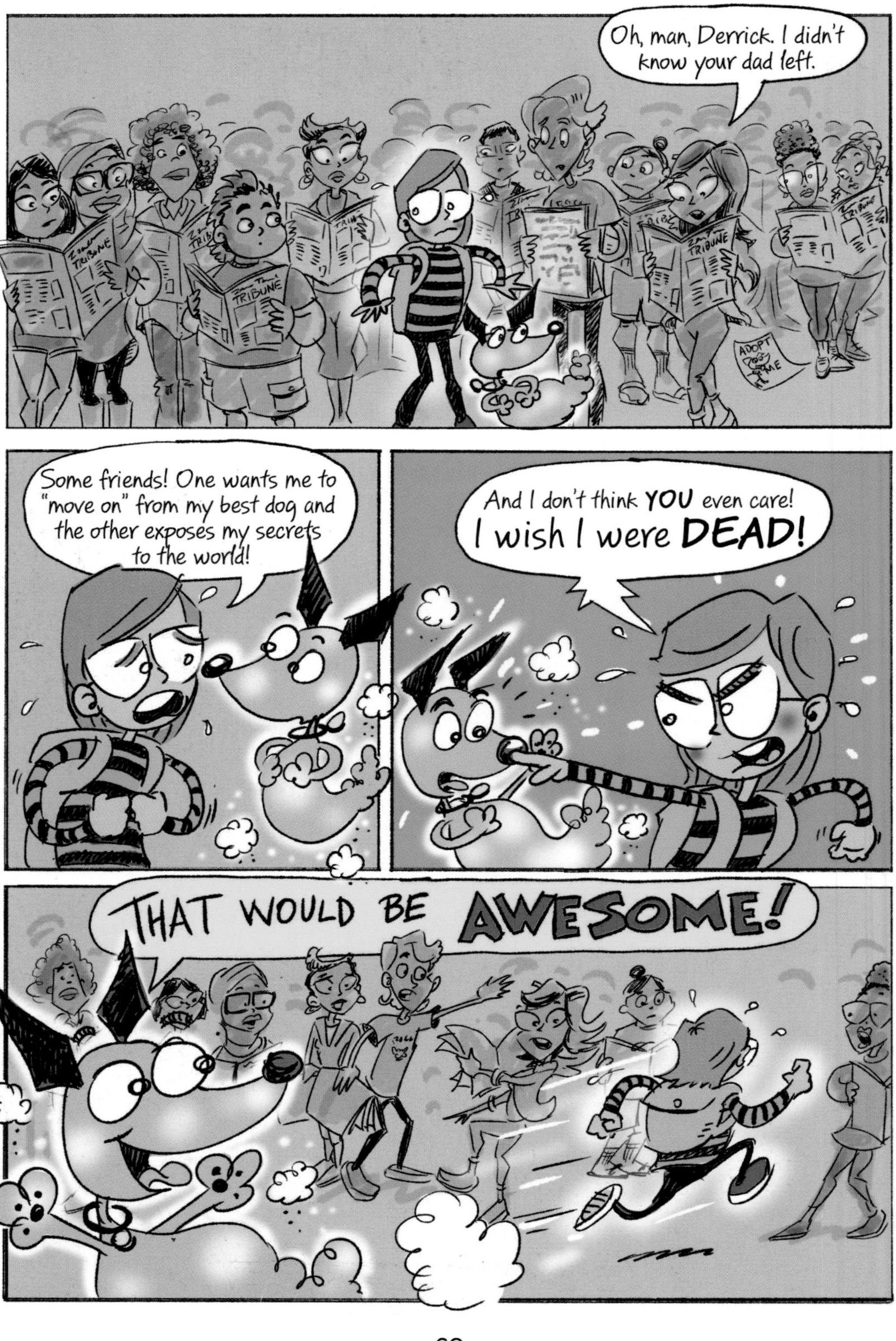
Oh, man, Derrick. I didn't know your dad left.
ADOPT ME
Some friends! One wants me to "move on" from my best dog and the other exposes my secrets to the world!
And I don't think YOU even care! I wish I were DEAD!
THAT WOULD BE AWESOME!

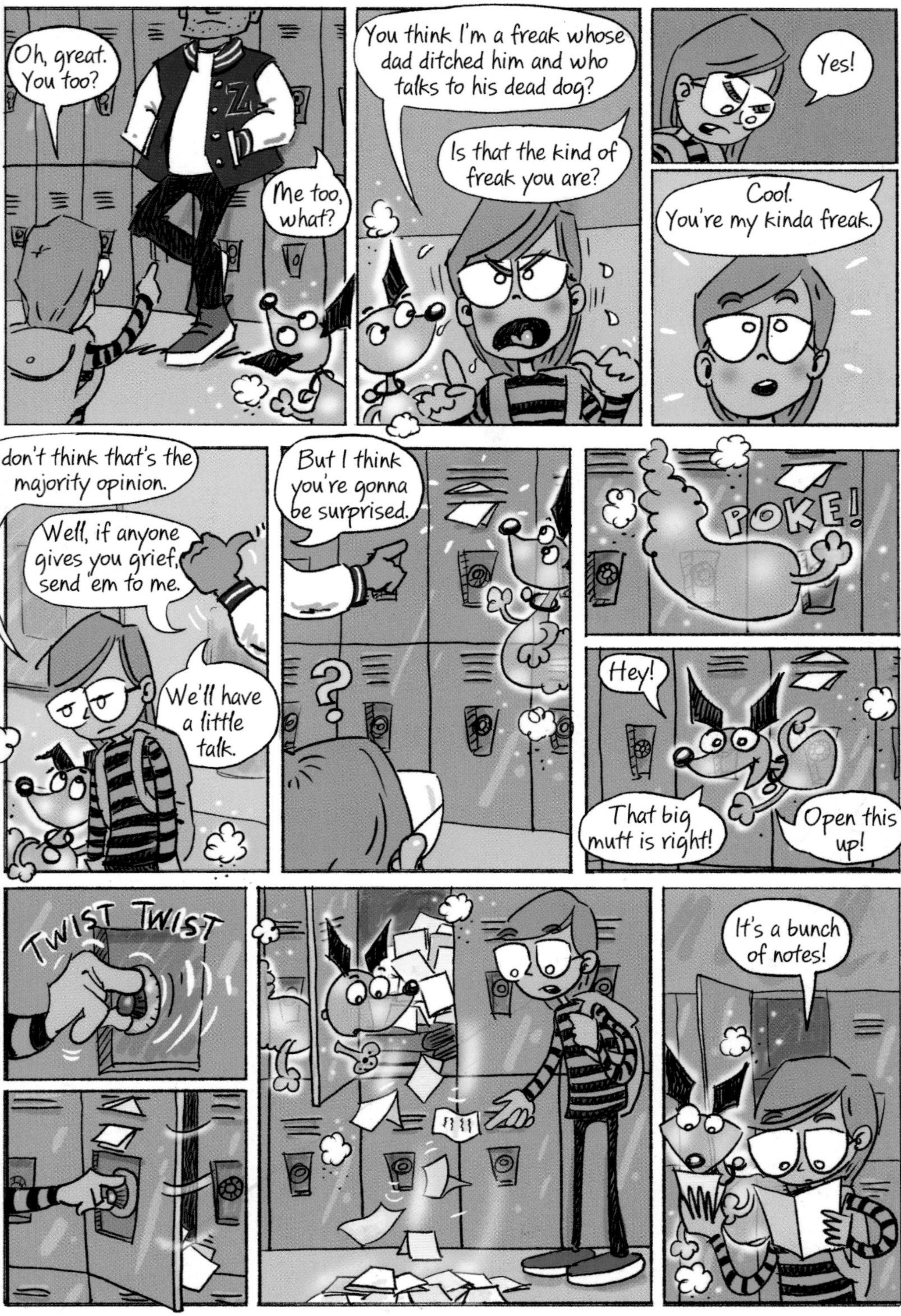
Oh, great. You too?
Me too, what?
You think I'm a freak whose dad ditched him and who talks to his dead dog?
Is that the kind of freak you are?
Yes!
Cool. You're my kinda freak.
don't think that's the majority opinion.
Well, if anyone gives you grief, send 'em to me.
We'll have a little talk.
But I think you're gonna be surprised.
?
POKE!
Hey!
That big mutt is right!
Open this up!
TWIST TWIST
It's a bunch of notes!

62

I'm sorry for going behind your back, but I really thought the school could use your comic.

And, you know, one of those notes is mine.

Well, the comic's out and it looks like I'm not the only weirdo at this school. So, we're cool.

And I'm sorry, too. I don't mean to rush you. I know you miss Max. Take your time.

Um. Er... Thanks.

This little guy needs a pack. It couldn't hurt to at least check him out.

And another dog could help me find that CAT!

the END

of DEAD MAX COMIX BOOK 1! STAY TUNED FOR BOOK 2: The ROCKING DEAD! —Dana & Max

Dana Sullivan grew up in Southern California drawing on every piece of paper he could find, especially his math homework. He kept at it until somebody finally published his books. He's written and illustrated a bunch—you can look 'em up if you don't believe it. He even teaches picture book and graphic novel classes.

Dana now lives near Seattle with his sweet wife, Vicki, and their two dogs: Bennie, who barks at the door a lot and takes Dana for a hike every day, and Max, who mostly stays in his urn. Dana's favorite color is dog and his favorite vegetable is peanut butter. See Dana's stuff, write him silly notes and send him even sillier drawings at www.danajsullivan.com.

Max and Dana know what it's like to be a kid going through stuff they don't want to share. But know this: **YOU ARE NOT ALONE**! Here are two excellent confidential resources:

Crisis Text Line: 741741 (USA) or 686868 (Canada) to connect with an online volunteer
National Suicide Prevention Lifeline: 1-800-273-TALK (8255) suicidepreventionlifeline.org